STO ✓

**FRIENDS
OF ACPL**

OPERATION NEPTUNE

OPERATION NEPTUNE

CHRISTOPHER NICOLE

HOLT, RINEHART & WINSTON
NEW YORK CHICAGO SAN FRANCISCO

Copyright © 1972 by Christopher Nicole • All rights reserved, including the right to reproduce this book or portions thereof in any form. Published simultaneously in Canada by Holt, Rinehart and Winston of Canada, Limited. ISBN: 0-03-091309-8 (Trade) • ISBN: 0-03-082310-1 (HLE) • Library of Congress Catalog Card Number: 76-182783 • Printed in the United States of America • First Edition. Designed by Kathleen F. Westray

BOOKS BY CHRISTOPHER NICOLE

OPERATION NEPTUNE
WHERE THE CAVERN ENDS
OPERATION MANHUNT
OPERATION DESTRUCT

The characters and events in this novel are invented; any resemblance to real persons or events is coincidental and unintended.

CONTENTS

Part One   The Hounds

Part Two   The Kill

OPERATION NEPTUNE

PART ONE

୬୬୬୬୬୬୬୬୬୬୬
THE HOUNDS

CHAPTER 1

The battered red saloon car rounded the corner in a long sideways lurch which carried it the width of the track before it straightened and hurtled forward again. Jonathan Anders moved his left hand from the wheel, first to change gears, then to flick a drip of sweat from his brow. His heart settled back into place, and he stared through the mud-caked windshield. Thorssen was perhaps a quarter of a mile in front, streaking down the long straight stretch.

Jonathan resisted the temptation to crouch over the wheel, to pretend he was dragging his car onward by his own strength; instead he sat well back, arms almost fully extended, hands tight on the wheel, correcting every tendency to skid on the slippery surface. In his early twenties, Jonathan was tall and slim, with good shoulders. He wore white overalls, and a crash helmet protected his dark brown hair. His wide mouth was a flat line as he braked and changed down for the next bend. The blue car of Thorssen had already disappeared, but as he came into the home stretch he saw his rival once again, and now he was sure he was closing the gap.

He flashed through the pits. David was holding up the board. Two laps to go, and a thumbs-up sign. In his single quick glance, Jonathan took in the stands and the advertisements, other cars—forced to retire from this race because of mechanical trouble, or awaiting the next event—and endless faces. The arena was far from full as yet; the main races, including the international Grand Prix, were not due to be staged until after lunch. Those spectators already here were the true enthusiasts, and although he could not hear them, Jonathan could *feel* their encouragement swelling toward him. In the two years he had been competing he had become a firm favorite with the local experts.

With only two laps to go, Jonathan drove his foot downward, and the car surged forward. Thorssen was sliding into the dogleg. If Thorssen had a weakness as a driver, it was this tendency to slide through the half bends; he invariably opened up a gap on the inside of the track. The dogleg was the place to take him. If you were close enough. Next time round would be the last opportunity.

Jonathan refused to brake at all. He took the bend at full throttle, inside wheels against the grass verge. The car began to move sideways, the tail swinging out, but he delayed correction until the last possible moment. Tires screaming, he hurtled into the next straight, while a huge "OOOH!" of combined horror and relief arose from the spectators. The red car moved right across the track once again, tail still waggling dangerously. But this was on the straight, and Jonathan had the time to let her settle down. And now he could see the flutter of the yellow scarf Thorssen wore round his neck.

Surprisingly, David was not waiting at the pits. Entering the last lap, and no interest from the crew? But he had no time to think about that now; there was Thorssen, and there was the dogleg. Jonathan drove his foot down once again. Thorssen was entering the bend, only yards in front; the smoke from his exhaust belched outward as he changed down. Once again Jonathan refused to brake, aimed his car at the inside of the track. Thorssen began his drift, and Jonathan saw the open space in front of him, the long length of the back straight. The red car leaped at the gap. Jonathan caught a glimpse of Thorssen's face, twisted with effort as he desperately tried to come back across. But it was too late. Jonathan was through, with an empty road in front, beginning the long skid he knew had to come, but which he was confident he could correct well before the next bend.

The noise seemed to come from very far away. Someone letting off a firecracker, perhaps in the crowd. Jonathan concentrated on getting the car straight once again. But he realized, first with surprise, and then with horror, that it was not going to respond quickly enough. There was a drag, and now he could smell a tremendous scorching, the scent of lifeless rubber being hauled over a tarred surface at a hundred miles an hour.

The noise had been a bursting tire. His tire. All thought of winning the race disappeared; it was now a simple matter of surviving the coming crash. He turned into the skid, instinctively, but the car was still traveling far too fast, and he knew he was going to swing right round. For an agonized moment he faced Thorssen, his own car traveling backward, and then the Norwegian was past him, sweeping on to victory.

Now Jonathan was right across the track and onto the bank, scything upward and still moving backward, while the spectators uttered a long wail of excited alarm and ran from the wooden railing at the top. This parted with a crack, and the car was at the top, and over. But at last losing momentum. The tires caught in the uneven surface, and the car turned round once again, now threatening to roll right over, while Jonathan swung the wheel to and fro in his efforts to keep the vehicle upright.

And then, so suddenly that he found this the most dazing event of all, the car was still, and quiet, only a faint hiss of steam seeping upward from the overworked radiator into the crisp autumn air. All the noise was outside, as people surged around him, pulling open doors, reaching in to see if he was hurt, shouting their relief and punctuating their cries with exclamations of "Bad luck!", presumably on having lost the race, and "Good luck!", for his escape from injury.

He allowed them to help him out, found he could stand unaided, pushed his goggles up on his forehead and took off his helmet. Faces passed in front of him, people seethed around him, but he did not really see them. He smiled mechanically, and declined offers of help without realizing what he was saying. Leaning against the car he watched Thorssen, having won the race, coming back around the track on his lap of honor. He raised his hand in salute and got a thumbs up in return. And here at last was David, freckle-faced and covered with grease as usual, clambering over the barrier to get to him.

"Jonathan? Are you all right?"

"I think so. Bit woozy."

"And the car?"

"Just a dead rear tire," Jonathan said. "And a few scratches, maybe. So far as I know."

"You just pushed her too hard," David said. "Just too hard. One day you're going to do yourself an injury."

Jonathan wasn't listening any more. He was watching another man approaching, who, having found it too difficult to get over the barrier, had elected to walk down to the break and come through that way. "Oh, blow," Jonathan said.

"Do you know that character?" David was bending over the car, releasing the hood to peer at the engine, sniffing for any telltale smells of scorching to indicate that something vital might have burned out. "Just appeared, he did, about ten minutes ago, and started asking all sorts of ridiculous questions."

"I know him." Jonathan stood up. "Good afternoon, Mr. Craufurd. What brings you to Brands Hatch?"

Craufurd took off his cap to fan himself. He was quite bald, except for a fringe of white hair above his ears. In a brilliantly checked pair of plus fours and a shooting jacket, he suggested a nineteenth-century squire who had been miraculously transported into the future, and did not entirely like what he found there. The suggestion was heightened by his stick, with which he tapped the ground like a bull preparing to charge, and by the contemptuous expression in his deceptively mild blue eyes as he surveyed the crowd, the car, and finally Jonathan.

"Do you know, for a moment back there I actually thought you were going to win."

"So did I," Jonathan admitted.

"And then, with equal certainty, I supposed that you were about to be killed, which would have meant an utterly wasted day. What went wrong?"

Jonathan kicked the rear wheel. "My tire blew out."

David straightened. "He was pushing her too hard. He can't get it through his head that a car is only an accumulation of metal and rubber. He thinks it's a part of himself."

"Pushing too hard," Craufurd said. "Yes. An admirable summing up, young man. Is he a relative of yours, Jonathan?"

"Just a friend. My mechanic."

Craufurd surveyed David's grease-stained fingers. "I won't shake your hand, if you don't mind. Jonathan, do you think you and I could go somewhere reasonably quiet and have a little chat?"

"I'll have to change," Jonathan said. "It won't take me long."

"Then do so, my dear boy. My car is in the park."

"Hey," David said. "You're not leaving right away, Jon?"

"I'm afraid I will have to," Jonathan said. "Have her towed back to the pit, will you, Dave? I'll try to contact you later."

"You'll try?" David demanded. "Just who is that old bird, anyway?"

"Mr. Craufurd?" Jonathan sighed. "I suppose you could say he's my employer. From time to time."

Craufurd indulged in a chauffeur-driven Rolls Royce. His driver was separated from the rest of the car by a glass partition, and in the back seat the head of the British Security Services relaxed in what could be described as a mini-office, complete with telephone and Dictaphone. It also contained a bar, from which he mixed himself a whisky and soda. "You don't drink spirits, do you, Jonathan?"

"I'm afraid I don't, Mr. Craufurd."

"Very wise. Very wise indeed."

"I wouldn't say no to a cold beer, though."

"Beer? Now that is something I do not stock." Craufurd lit a cigar, leaned back and surveyed the countryside. "I have always liked Kent. I have always found it peaceful. I had no idea that young men behaved like maniacs in decrepit motor cars right in the heart of such a beautiful county. What do you call your, ah, hobby?"

"Stock-car racing."

"And I gathered from your, ah, mechanic, that you are highly regarded by your various rivals?"

"Well, I don't know. I've won a few races. How did you know where to find me, Mr. Craufurd?"

"You may well ask." Craufurd sipped his drink, and seemed to feel better. "Your landlady suggested that you might be at Brands Hatch."

"But why you? I mean, where's Mr. Headly?"

"Otherwise engaged. And I can well understand

your concern. I imagine you intended to keep your, ah, sporting activities something of a secret. With good reason, my dear boy. Your instructions are to spend your spare time keeping as fit as possible, and preparing yourself, mentally and physically, for whatever calls your country, in the person of myself, may from time to time make upon you. So far as I am aware, at no time were you told to take a short course in suicide."

"It's not really dangerous," Jonathan protested. "I mean, it looks far worse than it is. And it does keep me fit, and teaches me to drive fast as well. You never know when that might come in handy."

"I fail to visualize such an occasion. If you ever drove like that on the public road you would wind up in court, and I should be very happy to see you there. I find the whole thing disturbing. I have for years been telling the Chancellor that my operatives are grossly underpaid and that recruitment is becoming increasingly difficult as the cost of living continues to rise. But if your salary permits you to maintain that junkheap at the risk of life and limb, I shall have to revise my opinion. There is another small matter, Jonathan. I do not, repeat not, approve of your racing activities, but *whenever* one of my people undertakes *any* course of action, I expect him, or her, to be totally successful. You did not win today."

"Well, my tire blew out. That's just bad luck, surely. I'd got my nose in front, and he wasn't going to come back again; he didn't have the time."

"My dear boy, I have been telling you for years that there is no such thing as luck. Your tire blew out either because it was slightly defective or was at an incorrect pressure, in which case the fault lies with your friend David, or because you were driving badly or recklessly, in which case the fault is entirely yours. Ponder that."

"I'm pondering the way we're going," Jonathan said. "This isn't the London road."

"We are not going to London. We are going to Gatwick Airport, where you will board an aircraft for Shannon. I have a ticket for you."

"But I haven't packed."

"Your suitcase is in the trunk. I told your landlady that I was your father, come to rescue you from your life of squalor behind the counter of that antiquarian bookshop."

"Oh. I thought I'd been forgotten."

"Which would be merely what you deserve. To be perfectly honest with you, Jonathan, now that the world, and certainly Great Britain, is endeavoring to live in a relatively peaceful fashion, discovering areas of activity in which someone with your attraction for trouble can usefully be employed is intensely difficult. I am not going to discuss that Scottish fiasco, which involved you in piracy, or that miniature gun battle in which you managed to become involved in the West Indies. I prefer to forget about them, to the best of my ability. Now, alas, circumstances entirely beyond my control have obliged me to use you once again in an overseas mission. But I do wish to impress upon you, Jonathan, that there is no possible reason for this to end in even fisticuffs, much less flying bullets, and no possible excuse will be accepted for such a misfortune."

Jonathan sighed. Craufurd had this unfortunate

tendency to be obscure. "And this is not going to happen somewhere in Ireland?"

"In Eire, to be precise. A country which has had more than its share of violence and misfortune during this century. I really regret most sincerely having to inflict you upon them, but as I said, I have no choice. I take it you read the newspapers?"

"From time to time."

"This one?" Craufurd reached into his briefcase, produced a folded copy of a national daily, four days old. "It is the second lead story."

Jonathan glanced at it. "I saw it."

"Did you read it?"

"Not very carefully. I didn't think it could possibly be of any interest to us."

"Then I wish you to read it now. Aloud. Take your time. We won't be at Gatwick for at least half an hour." Craufurd leaned back and closed his eyes.

Jonathan studied the page. " 'IRISH SENSATION,' " he read the headline. " 'WAS GEORGE HERRIES REALLY OTTO BENDERER?' "

And lower down. " 'Sensation came to the sleepy fishing village of Kiltone, in Western Eire, yesterday, following the funeral of publican George Herries, who died of a heart attack on Friday evening. For at the wake Kathleen Herries, widow of the deceased, announced that her husband was actually the famous German scientist Otto Benderer.

"In the thirties Benderer was Nazi Germany's leading physicist; and if Hitler could have been persuaded to go ahead with the development of atomic weapons instead of rockets, Benderer would have headed the project. With the abandonment of the atomic program, Benderer joined the German Navy, in which he had served, as a boy, in the First World War, this time with such success that he became one of the leading U-boat commanders in a very short space of time. In 1944 he was returned to a shore job. And in 1945 he was known to be working at a secret establishment in the north of Germany. What this new project involved has either never been discovered, or if it was discovered, has never been made public. But the American Air Force delivered one of its heaviest air raids on Oberglattau in January 1945, and completely destroyed the factory there, as well as Benderer's laboratory. From that moment not one word has been heard of Otto Benderer, and it was popularly supposed that he had been killed in the raid.

" 'Not so,' says Mrs. Herries. Otto had by then realized that the Third Reich was doomed, and he took advantage of the confusion caused by the raid to make his way across the Baltic into Sweden. He was an enthusiastic small boat sailor. From Sweden, after what Mrs. Herries calls 'unbelievable adventures,' he found his way into the Republic of Ireland and to the little village of Kiltone, which overlooks the restless Atlantic Ocean. There he settled into peaceful obscurity as publican George Herries. He spoke English fluently, and a slight German accent was neither unique nor a great handicap in Eire toward the end of the war.

" 'Did he take any notes or papers with him into hiding? Mrs. Herries doesn't know. She is much younger than her husband, and they never discussed his past. In fact, according to Mrs. Herries, after nineteen years of married life she only learned the truth about her husband shortly before his death. He had already suffered two heart attacks, and seemed to have suspected that his next might be his last, so he confessed everything to his wife.

" 'What *was* Otto Benderer working on when the American bombers struck Oberglattau? Was it another of the Fuehrer's secret weapons, which would have stopped the Allied advance and even at that late hour given Germany victory? This intriguing mystery was once again brought into focus by the death of this strange man, whose entire life was a secret.

"But the villagers of Kiltone recall that in the early afternoon, when his bar was closed, George Herries liked to make his way to the cliffs north of the harbor, sit there, and look out at the tumbling Atlantic rollers. Was he indeed Otto Benderer, ex-U-boat commander, ex-atomic wizard, dreaming about his past? Whatever George Herries' secret, or secrets, they are likely to remain just that, for the only man who could have told us the answer lies buried in Kiltone churchyard, close to the ocean he loved so well.' "

"There's a lot more blah as well," Jonathan said. "Do you want to hear right through to the end?"

"I think you've read enough," Craufurd said.

"I still don't see what could be interesting to us. So maybe this character Herries was Benderer. And maybe he wasn't. If we could have got hold of him when he was still alive we might have got somewhere. But as it is . . ."

"He's dead, and there's an end to the matter. I couldn't agree with you more, my dear boy. Or perhaps I should say, I would not have agreed with you more, had not yesterday a contingent of Russian journalists descended upon the unfortunate village of Kiltone. To do a story on Otto Benderer."

"So? They're quite hipped on Nazi scientists, aren't they? Sometimes I think they're still busy fighting the last one."

"Unfortunately, we have to assume that they also are thinking in terms of having to fight the next one as well. Aren't we all, my dear boy? I could understand *Pravda* sending a journalist to Eire, to do a piece on a very, very old man, who was once quite famous. But four? No, no, only one of that group can be a legitimate journalist, Jonathan. The rest are looking for something."

"For what, for instance?"

"Who knows."

"But you would like me to find out."

"I would indeed. You will also travel as a journalist, and I have here all the necessary documents to confirm your occupation. Even a union card. Now do please try to understand that I have no desire for you to enter into any cloak and dagger activities, or even to do any sleuthing. I do not feel that those aspects of our work are really your strengths. However, should you find it possible to use your undoubted charm on Kathleen Herries, and perhaps come back with something belonging to Otto Benderer, any notebook, any scrap of paper with writing or figures on it, however indecipherable it may seem to you, I shall be your friend for life. On the other hand, I must insist that should you get into any trouble whatsoever with these Russians, as you are so prone to do, you need not bother to come back at all, as I shall take a very, very dim view of your present, as well as your future, in my organization."

"Oh, great," Jonathan said. "You're pitchforking me into the middle of a haystack when you're not even sure there's a needle to be found."

"Oh, no," Craufurd said. "I'm quite sure there's a needle around, Jonathan. The newspaper was right in one respect, for sure. Neither ourselves nor the Americans ever did find out what was going on at Oberglattau. That factory belonged to a munitions firm and was lucky to have escaped destruction earlier in the war. And it was utterly destroyed. But once the Allied troops got there, on their advance through Germany, seeing that it had contained Otto Benderer's old laboratory, they gave it a thorough going over. They found nothing, except the remains of large, enormous tanks deep in the basement of the factory."

"Tanks can mean anything."

"These had special ducts for introducing salt water from the Baltic into them. Tanks the size of a large house. That suggests underwater, under-ocean experiments of some kind. And Otto Benderer was a U-boat captain in his spare time, remember? And George Herries used to spend all his time sitting on a hillside and staring at the sea. I think there are sufficient links present to suggest that Herries and Benderer are indeed the same man. Were, I should say."

"And the Russians know what he was up to, in 1945?"

"We have to face it, Jonathan; their spy system, in Germany, at any rate, was far more efficient than ours, both before and during the last war. No doubt because they never had any doubt at all that they would have to fight Nazi Germany; whereas we always hoped to be able to live with them. Incorrectly, as it turned out.

"Now that was a very heavy raid on Oberglattau, certainly. But it didn't kill Benderer, so there is no reason to suppose that it killed everybody else in the place either. Suppose one of those survivors was a Russian agent? Or even that he was a scientist taken prisoner by the Russians when Germany finally collapsed, and who agreed to work for them? We know there were quite a few of those. This would be someone who knew what Benderer was working on, but had no access to his secret laboratory or his files. So the Kremlin, with Benderer apparently dead and his laboratory utterly destroyed, would have said, well, there's a stroke of bad luck. But the Kremlin, like the elephant, never forgets. So twenty-five or more years later the name Otto Benderer crops up again, and the Kremlin is on to it like a dog on a bone. We must beat them to it, Jonathan."

"One lonely Englishman," Jonathan said sadly. "And four large Russians."

"Ah, but the Irish, my dear boy, are practically our own kith and kin. You don't want to forget that. And besides, they speak our language."

The guidebook said: "Sligo Bay is in reality a southward arm of the Bay of Donegal itself, famous in song and story. Here is as wild and beautiful a part of Eire as can be discovered, where only a scattering of offshore islands stands between Ireland and the great Atlantic rollers. As may be expected, the coast itself is sparsely populated, and indeed the tiny fishing village of Kiltone stands almost isolated, although situated only a few miles from Sligo itself."

Which sounded attractive enough. But first thing was to get to Sligo, and it is a train journey of several hours from the airport at Shannon to the northern town; it occurred to Jonathan that he was not likely to reach his destination much before nightfall.

"Ye'll have come for the fox hunting," suggested the conductor.

"I've never done it," Jonathan confessed. "I've always rather been on the side of the fox."

"Ye're English," the conductor accused. "Sligo, is it?"

"Well, actually, I'm trying to get to Kiltone."

The conductor gazed at him, brows drawn together over a long nose. "Kiltone, ye say? Then ye don't want to go all the way into town, ye don't. Ye get off . . . ah, never mind. I'll tell ye when."

Which might prove an advantage, Jonathan decided. Meanwhile, he could sit back and admire the green of the countryside, even in October, and try to get his thoughts straight. Craufurd had this habit of descending out of the blue and whipping his operatives away to the farthest corner of the earth, without either a warning or an apology.

Not that Eire could be considered the farthest corner of the earth, by any means. Amazing to think that only this morning he'd been driving at Brands Hatch. But actually he was flattered. His career *had,* as Craufurd had suggested, been somewhat checkered. So much so that in recent months he had been wondering if he might not have made a mistake in his choice of vocations. But it had all seemed so much like a dream come true, once.

He remembered his lonely boyhood, compounded by the early death of his mother, after which he had had to go to school in England while his father had pursued a diplomatic career in all corners of the globe. This was romantic, certainly. Dad was now British consul in one of the South American countries, and could look forward to a distinguished career at ambassadorial level. But he had seen less and less of his son in recent years, and assumed that, after a not very successful university career, Jonathan had quietly dropped out and gone to work as a bookseller's assistant in the West End of London.

Instead of which he had gone to work for Craufurd. He had actually been doing quite well at the university, had got a half blue for chess and a full blue for athletics, had looked forward to a B.A. degree without yet having any clear idea of what he wanted to do with his life, when he had met Harold Indman. The introduction had been arranged by one of the tutors, who he now realized must have been in Indman's confidence, if not in his employ. Indman had been on a visit to the university, ostensibly, and wanted a game of chess. Why not let him try his wits against the university champion? But they had only played one game. Indman had preferred to talk, about Jonathan, and his background. And most of all about his future.

"It is difficult, isn't it, nowadays," he had said. "Everything is so regimented, so controlled, so surrounded by rules and regulations, by established steps in a ladder, I can quite see that the future can be difficult for an ambitious young man without a burning urge to do any one particular thing. Have you ever considered working for the Country?"

"You must be joking."

"I don't mean the Civil Service, you know. I don't even mean the Diplomatic Service. But it occurs to me that a young man like yourself, young and fit and quick-witted, and not exactly hampered by family ties, might both enjoy and do very well at what I have in mind."

"Which is what, exactly, Mr. Indman?"

It had meant leaving the university and going to work in Indman's bookshop, theoretically on a trial basis. This had been his cover. In reality it had meant learning to shoot and learning unarmed combat and learning to break and enter and learning to code and to decode and to use people, and places, and things, to the ultimate. It had meant meeting people like Michael Headly, and liking them, and ultimately being proud of belonging to the same organization. It had meant becoming used to existing in an entirely new world, where there were no trade unions and no police, at least, no police on your side, and no rules and no assistance to be expected from anyone except your known colleagues. It had suggested danger and excitement, combined with a slight air of lawlessness. And it had always had an out, for three years. He had supposed.

But after only eighteen months he had met Craufurd, and had been asked to carry out a very small assignment. That had exploded in his face, had involved him in a contest of wits with Anna Cantelna which had very nearly cost him his life. He remembered her with a strange mixture of awe and pleasure. Awe, because she was a Nobel Prize winner, one of the greatest of Russian scientists and of all marine biologists, anywhere, and at the same time a dedicated and ruthless Communist, devoted only to the aggrandizement of Mother Russia; and pleasure, because he *had* beaten her in the end, and she had been such a charming and attractive woman, even behind her deadliness —and he had a sneaking suspicion she had rather liked him.

But Craufurd had not been amused. The incident had caused questions in the House, apparently induced the old blighter to regard his newest recruit as someone to be used only in an emergency.

This unfortunate point of view had been confirmed by the West Indian business. Jonathan refused to accept any responsibility for the hurricane and all that had followed it in the way of mayhem, but on the other hand, had he not led with his chin, in complete defiance of instructions, he would never have been on board the doomed schooner at all.

Now, presumably, he was being given a third chance to prove that he was capable of being a truly discreet, capable operative. All he had to do was ask one or two questions, make sure these people *were* Russian agents, and then go home again. So maybe there was no need to be flattered, after all. Craufurd had chosen him for this particular assignment because not even Jonathan Anders could possibly mess it up. There's nothing like feeling your superiors have confidence in you.

"Ye'll want to get off at the next station." The conductor appeared in the doorway. "It's a small one, but ye'll be the only passenger. There's a taxi, always meets the train. He'll see ye to Kiltone."

"Thanks very much." Jonathan hooked his bag off the rack as the train began to slow. It certainly was a small station, and looked the more gloomy in the dusk, as the sun had just disappeared behind the hills.

"Ye'll be wanting to go to Kiltone," said a little young man, wearing a porkpie hat.

"As a matter of fact, yes," Jonathan agreed.

"English, are ye?" remarked the taxi driver, and relieved Jonathan of his suitcase. "I've a cousin in England. London, or some such place."

"Have you now." Jonathan got into the back of the car. It wasn't a recent model.

"Well, it's hard to say exactly." The taxi driver started the engine, and they drove out of the station yard. "He's moved around from time to time. He's in prison, ye'll understand."

"I'm very sorry to hear that."

"Ah, it's his own fault. He was incompetent." The taxi driver pronounced each syllable as if it were a separate word. "Blowing up a post office, he was after, and he missed the building entirely. They'll have to let him out, eventually." He sounded unhappy at the prospect.

Jonathan gazed out of the window. They seemed to be driving over some kind of moorland, as near as he could see. But he figured they were fairly high up, and already the breeze had the sting, and the force, of the sea wind; of course, right here there was nothing between Ireland and America. And just over there, much closer at hand, was an enormous square building with a crenelated roof.

"What on earth is that?" he asked.

"Sure, that's Kiltone Castle."

"But there are lights burning. Is it inhabited?"

"Oh, yes, by them foreigners. Well, they're English, ye'll understand. They own the place. There's a right United Nations up there, now."

Jonathan pondered that one. "I'm not with you."

"Ah, ye don't want to go up there, ye don't. Ye'll be staying the night?"

"I had intended to. Is there a hotel in Kiltone?"

"Now what would we be doing with a hotel in Kiltone? Ye'll be a reporter?"

"As a matter of fact, yes."

"Ah, then ye'll want to be staying at the inn, won't ye?"

"Will I?"

"Mind ye, ye've missed all the goings on, really. The man's dead, and there's an end to it. If he was anyone of importance. I'll tell ye this: Many's the glass of beer I've had with George Herries, and never a word about no U-boats. Ah, Kathy Herries is a sweet child. I wouldn't like ye to think anything but that. But she's given to gossip. Ay, yes. This is Kiltone."

The road wound down off the moor into a single cobbled street, lined with stone cottages, not one of which, Jonathan estimated, could have been built in this century. The almost equally ancient taxi banged and rattled its way over the uneven surface, down to the diminutive harbor. Jonathan had been in places like Guernsey, where there are harbors only big enough for fishing smacks; this one appeared even smaller. Beyond the tiny stone breakwater, however, a high bluff protruded out to sea and afforded some shelter from the ocean; there several fishing craft rode to their moorings.

"Here ye are," said the taxi driver. "The Kiltone Arms. I won't come in. Ye just tell Kathy that Tim dropped ye off. She'll see ye right. And then ye can ask her all your questions over a glass of beer."

"Thanks very much." Jonathan paid him, took his suitcase to the door, cautiously pushed it open. He stood in a small lobby, containing two large pots filled with what appeared to be miniature palm trees, and off which opened three doors. The one on the right was clearly the public bar; it was a blaze of light and filled with noise and the clink of glasses. But he did not wish his arrival in Kiltone to be any more public than it already promised to be.

He tried the left-hand door and just as hastily closed it again; there were three men in there, talking together in low voices and drinking whisky. They wore overcoats and had not troubled to remove their hats. He thought it might be rather amusing if he and the Russians all sat down to dinner together. But he wanted a chance to see Mrs. Herries first.

He opened the center door, found himself in a dark hallway. On his left was a flight of steps, with a landing halfway up, and on his right a small table, on which there lay a book and a bell. He rang this, waited for a moment and watched the door at the end of the hall open.

She was a pretty, dark-haired girl with freckles and an upturned nose. She wore an apron over a short dress and slip-on sandals. "Yes?"

"Mrs. Herries?" Jonathan asked in surprise.

"Miss Herries. My name is Joan." She came toward him, suddenly efficient. "Ye'll be wanting a room?"

"If there is one."

"Aye. Aye." She opened the book, glanced at him as she sat down. "For the one night?"

"Well, I don't know. Can't we leave it open?"

"No reason why not." She gazed at him, frowning slightly. "What name will it be?"

"Anders. Jonathan Anders."

She wrote carefully, seemed satisfied. "Will ye sign, Mr. Anders?"

He obeyed.

"Now, if ye'll come with me." She led him up the stairs. She had pretty legs, too. And her father had been a high-ranking German physicist. Perhaps. What a remarkable world it was.

He followed her along a corridor. There appeared to be four bedrooms, and he was shown to the last. She opened the door for him, stood back. "Will this do ye?"

The room was not very large, and contained a four-poster bed, a table, a chair, and an old-fashioned washstand with a china ewer and basin. "It looks charming," Jonathan said.

"Ye'll be wanting supper?"

"If it's no trouble."

"No trouble at all. We eat at seven. In the back room."

"Oh. Oh, yes. Thanks very much. I'll be there."

"And the bathroom is just along the hall." She continued to gaze at him. Hostilely? He couldn't be sure. "A reporter, are ye?"

"I suppose you've seen too many of those."

"Too many," she agreed. "Too many. Supper in half an hour, Mr. Anders."

She closed the door. What a strange girl. Why? Because she was fed up with nosy reporters trying to make capital out of her mother? Far better to think, what a pretty girl. He wondered who else was staying in the hotel? The three Russians, supposing he was right about them? But he had only counted four doors, including his own, and Craufurd had said there were *four* Russian agents. If they were living here he'd have expected Joan Herries to tell him the inn was full.

Then there was the miniature United Nations up at the castle, as Tim the taxi driver had put it. There were things to be learned here, all right. But at least the Russians were still around. They hadn't yet got what they had come for.

He stood at the window, watched the street for awhile, saw the taxi slowly bumping its way over the cobbles, coming from the harbor. He wondered if anyone had been out fishing today. If anyone did anything in Kiltone. Apart from the taxi, there was no one around, and the village was for the moment dark —although from the glow beyond the hills he did not think it would be very long before the full moon would be doing its bit.

The taxi stopped outside the pub, and Tim got out and went inside. He had decided to have his drink after all. Jonathan opened his suitcase, took out his dressing gown and went along to the bathroom. It had been a very long day, and he figured he just had the time for a hot tub. Just. It took several minutes for the slow drip of hot water from the geyser to fill the bath, and by then it was starting to run cold. So he abandoned any idea of a long soak and had a quick dip instead. At least it made him feel better. He thought he would have dinner, and then a chat with Mrs. Herries, and then an early night. Much depended on what Mrs. Herries was prepared to tell him, on what she had already told the Russians. Presumably he had to stay in Kiltone for as long as they did. But he rather liked the idea of that. The village looked well worth exploring, and there was Joan Herries, for all her hostility. And in the line of duty, too; Joan would surely have something to tell about her father.

He whistled softly to himself as he walked back along the cordidor. He felt distinctly tired. He was even beginning to wonder if his chat with Kathleen Herries couldn't wait until tomorrow. He'd have a good supper and go to bed, and tomorrow. . . He opened the door of his bedroom and the whistle died as he gazed at the scene of utter destruction in front of him.

"What the . . ." He started across the room, and entered a world of blackness.

CHAPTER 2

Consciousness returned slowly. Jonathan did not really want to open his eyes. There was too much pain out there, waiting to get in.

But someone was bathing his forehead with gentle, insistent fingers. Reluctantly he raised his eyelids, and at the same moment inhaled a familiar scent. Joan Herries knelt on the floor, and his head was pillowed on her lap, while she dabbed at his hair with a piece of cotton wool which stank of liniment. "Whisht," she said, as she saw he was awake. "I'm glad to see ye back in the land of the living, Mr. Anders, that I am."

"You can say that again," said another voice, and Jonathan tried to turn his head. This was a young man, not very tall and somewhat thin as well, who wore horn-rimmed spectacles and a pleasant smile. "Hi," he said. "You were so completely gone ten seconds back we thought you *were* gone."

"But what happened?"

"Ye must have had your bath too hot," Joan

Herries suggested. "And fainted just after ye got back to your room. Then ye must have hit your head when ye fell. Why, I've no idea at all how long ye must have lain here, but when ye did not come down for dinner, I came looking for ye. And a mighty nasty shock I had, too."

"So she called me," said the young man. "Not wanting to disturb her mother. Mrs. Herries has had more than enough excitement these last few days."

Jonathan sat up, remembered to straighten his dressing gown. "You're American," he said.

"Guilty. Pete Rodgers. No relation to anyone of importance, musically or diplomatically. I'm your fellow prisoner, in Joan's keeping."

"Now, is that a nice thing to say, Mr. Rodgers?" Joan asked. "Mr. Anders is in your line of business, too."

"I thought we might be after the same thing," Jonathan said. "You didn't by any chance dot me one as well, did you, old man?"

"Say again?"

"Now, ye take it easy, Mr. Anders," Joan said. "Ye're going to be a little unsteady for a while."

Jonathan reached his feet, discovered she was right. He sat on the bed just in time to stop himself falling across it and waited for the room to stop spinning.

"What the man needs is a drink," Rodgers said.

"A nip of whisky," Joan said. "I'll get it with his dinner. It's waiting, Mr. Anders. All our dinners are waiting."

"You don't seem to understand," Jonathan said. "I didn't faint from a hot bath, or anything like that.

Someone was waiting for me, and he hit me as I came through the door."

"The Wild West comes to Kiltone," Rodgers suggested.

"Now, really, Mr. Anders, why should anyone wish to hit ye on the head?" Joan asked. "And ye a stranger here and all."

"He was searching my room," Jonathan explained. "I must have come back sooner than he thought I would. Yes, of course. The water in the bath ran cold, so I had a quick dip and came back. And everything was in a mess. My clothes were strewn all over the place, and . . ." He gazed at the foot of the bed. The suitcase lay where he had left it. It was closed, and the only things of his in sight were those he had worn on the journey from England, neatly folded across the back of a chair. "Who tidied up?"

"Tidied up, Mr. Anders?"

Jonathan started to scratch his head, hurriedly changed his mind.

"It's being in Ireland," Rodgers explained. "Something in the air. Makes you feel like a new man. Or an old one. Sometimes."

"Okay," Jonathan decided. "I suppose you must be right. I must have tripped, as you said, and fallen. I'll be down as soon as I'm dressed."

"Now, ye're sure ye're feeling all right, Mr. Anders?" Joan asked anxiously.

"Feeling better every second," Jonathan promised her, quite untruthfully.

"Well, then, let's eat," Rodgers said. "Before everything is stone cold."

Jonathan watched them leave, then he closed the

door and checked his suitcase. It was unlocked. But of course he had unlocked it to take out his dressing gown. He opened the bag, looked inside. But he hadn't actually packed it, and he didn't know how tidy Craufurd had been.

He was quite sure he hadn't tripped. And it had been only a few minutes ago. He should have started worrying the moment he'd got off the train. Everything had been running just a shade too smoothly.

Hurriedly he dressed, closed the door behind him, very softly, and tiptoed to the stairs. The hall was, as before, dark and deserted. He went downstairs, testing each step for a creak, and through the door into the lobby, throwing open the door of the saloon bar. The Russians were gone, and in their place, in the farthest corner, a young couple was whispering together over a couple of drinks. They jerked upright and stared at him.

"I'm sorry," Jonathan said, and closed the door behind him. But how could it have been one of the Russians? They didn't even know he was here, yet.

Come to think of it, who *had* known he had arrived?

Save Joan. Which was ridiculous. And even if it wasn't ridiculous, but rather obvious, *she* couldn't possibly have hit him. So she had to have an accomplice. Pete Rodgers? Now there was a likely possibility. Then they needn't have left the bedroom at all, just finished their search, repacked his suitcase, and started the hospital scene.

Which made him feel very unhappy. His first impression of each of them had been entirely favorable. And why on earth should Joan want to do such a thing? She couldn't have laid out every reporter who'd come to see her mother. Not unless she was some kind of maniacal black widow spider.

No, far more promising to think about was Tim the taxi driver. Tim often had a drink with Mrs. Herries when he brought a fare. But this night he had refused to stop. And then he'd come back as soon as he'd figured Jonathan would be safely inside.

He opened the door to the public bar, paused to become accustomed to the light, the haze of cigarette smoke, the cessation of noise at his entry. There were twelve people in here, nine men and three women. The men wore flat caps and topcoats, and the women were in headscarves and vast shawls. They were drinking beer, and someone had been playing a flute, but this had come to a sudden stop at the appearance of a stranger.

And not one of them looked under forty years old. Didn't they have any young people in Kiltone other than Joan Herries and the couple in the other room?

"Ye'll be Mr. Anders," said the woman behind the bar. "Joannie told me another one had arrived."

"Mrs. Herries?" She certainly was an older edition of Joan, but there was too much color in her cheeks. Clearly she had been drowning her sorrows, and the bright flush was set off by her black dress.

"That's me," she said. "So come in and have yourself a drink. Don't just stand there, man. Whisht. But what happened to your head? There's a great lump of sticking plaster and all."

"I had a slight fall." Jonathan crossed the room, and the locals recommenced their drinking, talking in much lower tones than before. But the flute player remained silent, and Jonathan had no doubt they were all watching him.

"What'll it be?" Mrs. Herries asked.

"You wouldn't have a cold beer, by any chance?"

"Cold? Bottled, ye mean? Man, ye're in the wrong bar. But I've a very nice draft lager here, and it's chilled. Ye try a drop of that, Mr. Anders. That'll stop your head spinning." She leaned on the handle, and the liquid frothed into the glass. "Man, ye're late. Did ye know that? They was thick as flies round here at the beginning of the week. Reporters, I mean." She sighed. "Now there's just them Russian characters and our nice Mr. Rodgers. But he's only here for the hunting, worse luck."

"The hunting?"

"The foxes, Mr. Anders. The foxes. Oh, we've a big hunt here in Kiltone. The hounds belong to the old lord, up on the hill. Ye must have seen the castle."

"I did indeed. And it belongs to a lord?"

"An *English* lord. There's your beer. Ah, ye must have heard of him. Lord Wantage, his name is. Lives there all alone in that great pile, save for his daughter. All they do is ride and hunt. Right proper gentry, ye'd think. Wouldn't ye think that, Mr. Anders?"

"I would, indeed. And Mr. Rodgers has come for the hunt, you say?"

"I doubt he'll ride. He's come to do a piece, that's what I said. Tomorrow is the first meet of the season. It's a big occasion in these parts, ye'll understand. Everyone in Kiltone attends the first day of the hunt. And then it's open house at the castle afterward. Oh, his lordship is a proper gentleman, ye'll have to allow that. Mr. Rodgers is here from *Time* or *Life* or one of them posh magazines. Man, ye should just see his camera. Now, if he'd only come about the other business, he'd make me an offer. Oh, yes."

Jonathan drank some beer, and felt better. "An offer? For what?"

Mrs. Herries laid one finger on her nose and winked. "Man, ye're a cute one, Mr. Anders. Ain't ye here for the very same thing? But seeing as how ye are, and staying in me house and all, I'll put ye in the picture, as ye might say. When I told that young man from Dublin that dear old George was really Professor Benderer, it was all a bit of a giggle, really. It was the truth, mind. Oh, yes. I never told a lie in me life. Well, not more than now and then. And it was all George's idea. You break the news once I'm six feet under, he'd say to me. You tell them, Kathy girl. That's what he always called me, ye know. Kathy girl. Oh, he was a one. I'd always known he was somebody, ye know, Mr. Anders. Ye can always tell. He was restless, especially as he grew older. Ye know what I think? I think he figured he never got his rightful due from the world. And that he didn't. Oh, he must have been great once. He was great when I knew him. We were happy, Mr. Anders, I can tell ye that, and proud I am to have been his wife. But I did what he told me to do. Ye tell them, Kathy, he'd say, and watch them all go wild. So I did like he said, and he was right. But I never realized there'd be anything in it for me, except maybe a bit of publicity for the old house. And then this Russian comes along yesterday and offers me money, he does."

"For the story?" Jonathan asked.

"What story, Mr. Anders? I told the whole story to that young fellow from Dublin. No, this Russkie says he wants to do a whole biography on dear old George, right back when, and he wanted any papers, letters, everything I might have in George's handwriting. D'ye know, he even wanted to open up the coffin and take photographs of poor old George lying there all peaceful like? Wanted me permission, he did. But it was the papers he was after, really. Offered me money for them. Good money."

"And you sold your papers to him?"

Kathleen Herries smiled, a slow widening of her generous mouth which at the same moment brought an immense sparkle to her eyes. "Now, why would I be after doing anything like that, Mr. Anders? George didn't leave no papers."

"Not even a letter?"

"Not even a letter. Dear old George didn't *leave* a single solitary thing behind him, saving only this pub. I told that Russkie he was wasting his time."

"But he's still here."

"I figure maybe he didn't believe me. He was back again this evening, asking me if I was sure I hadn't forgotten something. Asking if he could maybe have a search of me house. Well, I told him a thing or two, and I can tell ye that, Mr. Anders. Search me house, indeed! I told him I'd have the constables on him if he tried any more foolishness with me. Had a couple of his friends with him, too. So I told him to have a drink and push off."

"You mean they're not staying here?"

"Oh, no," Kathleen Herries said. "I wouldn't have them Commies in my house. They're staying up at the castle with his lordship."

Jonathan finished his beer. "Let me get this straight," he said. "The Russian party is staying at the castle with Lord Wantage?"

"And his stuck-up daughter, and all. Oh, yes, Mr. Anders." Kathleen Herries giggled. "Maybe they're waiting on for the meet. Can ye imagine it, Mr. Anders? Three great big commissars, and the woman, charging about in toppers and red coats? That'd suit them, wouldn't ye say?"

"The woman?"

"Oh, they've a woman with them. Old friend of his lordship's, so they say. But ye look here, Mr. Anders, are ye having another? Because if ye do, ye'll be after missing supper, and that'll annoy Joannie. Right proud of her cooking, she is, and a right virago she can be when it's spoiled."

"Oh. Oh, yes. I suppose I'd better eat."

"Ye can come this way, seeing as ye're a guest." Kathleen Herries opened the hatch in the bar. "Just through that door."

Jonathan discovered himself beyond the door before he was quite sure what was happening. But come to think of it, he wasn't at all sure what was happening anywhere. Craufurd had said to keep out of trouble and ask a few quiet questions. The old geezer hadn't said anything about what to do if you were knocked on the head. Or about members of the British aristocracy who entertained Russian operatives at home.

And what had Mrs. Herries meant by saying, "He didn't *leave* anything?"

"Well, hi." Pete Rodgers was tackling an outsize portion of apple pie. "Is the condemned man going to eat a hearty meal?"

Jonathan sat down. "Where's Joan?"

"Sharpening her little ax, I should think. If you don't mind a word of advice, Anders, when in Ireland —in real Ireland, as opposed to the tourist villages— you want to do like the natives do. And one of the things the natives do is show a proper appreciation of the good things of life, like cooking. And Joan is a very good cook. And she knows it. She went upstairs to look for you, when you didn't show all over again, and was quite upset when you weren't there. But when she took a look through the window behind the bar, and saw you drinking beer and chatting with her mother, she damn near blew her top."

"I'll apologize," Jonathan promised. "I didn't mean to upset her." What *about* Pete Rodgers? In his company, it was impossible to suppose he could have lurked behind a door with a blackjack. Anyway, didn't Jonathan Anders always lead with his chin? He didn't figure it could do anything but good in this instance. "The fact is, Rodgers, I wasn't fooling upstairs. Someone did land me one. And I mean to find out who."

"Oh, come now." But Rodgers frowned. "You're *not* kidding, are you? But why?"

"That's another thing I want to find out. When exactly did Joan call you?"

"I didn't look at my watch. I was in the bar, having a beer before dinner. She did it very quietly.

Didn't want to upset her mum, you see. But look here, you're not thinking she had anything to do with it? I may as well warn you that in the twenty-four hours I've been here I've become just a little partial to that young lady."

"Twenty-four hours," Jonathan said. "For the hunting, you say?"

"It starts tomorrow. You know something, you have a complex."

"Yeah. Well, I'll lay you a little bet that the first time someone bats you over the head, you'll have a slight complex too. Oh, hi, Joan." Hurriedly he got to his feet, and Rodgers did likewise.

She wore a reefer jacket over her dress, and her head was tied up in a green scarf. "So ye've decided to eat," she remarked. "Well, ye'll have to serve yourself. Mum'll give ye a drop of the hard stuff, if ye're so minded."

"I'll manage," Jonathan said. "Without the hard stuff, if it's all right by you."

"Suit yourself. I'm going out. I wouldn't be surprised if your food isn't ice cold by now." She banged the hall door behind her.

"You brought it on yourself," Rodgers said. "The food's in the oven."

"The devil with that," Jonathan said. "I'll be seeing you."

"*Just* one minute. Where do you think you're going?"

"Out."

"You're figuring on following Joan?"

"She's my only lead. Heck, she's one of the only

two people who knew I was here when I caught one."

"I told you, you have a complex. And Joan is probably off to meet her young man. They don't want you barging in."

"That's something else that's bothering me. Apart from a couple in the saloon bar, there just don't seem to *be* any young people in this village. This is the only pub. So where are they all?"

"Down at the discotheque."

"Which is where?"

Pete Rodgers scratched his head. "Come to think of it, there isn't one. I wonder what the young people of Kiltone do for kicks?"

"I aim to find out."

"So wait a moment." Pete crammed a last mouthful of pie into his mouth, hurried behind Jonathan. "You know that girl *can* cook?"

"Then stay and have mine as well," Jonathan suggested.

"Not on your life. You have a mean look in your eye. I want to be there whenever you manage to catch up with Joan."

Which, presuming she *was* involved, might not be a bad idea, Jonathan decided; it would at least decide once and for all whether or not Pete was involved as well. This was one of those times when a good hard think might provide one or two answers. But thinking would have to wait until he had the time.

The moon had risen, and the village was a glow of light, except where the houses cast black shadows. But the street was empty. And windswept.

"Brrr!" Pete said. "You've lost her. Let's go have a beer."

"What about up there?" Jonathan asked.

On the north side of the little harbor the cliff climbed steeply, and in the brilliant moonlight a woman in a headscarf was clearly visible as she made her way up the path. "Now, why should she be taking a walk up there, all on her lonesome, on a rather cold night?"

"For pity's sake, but you Limeys are backward," Pete remarked. "She's going to meet someone, that's what. And she won't want us around."

"Okay," Jonathan said. "Okay. So I give you my word that the moment she gets a lover's welcome, I'll push off. I just want to see her get it. Come on." He ran across the street into the shelter of the houses on the far side.

Pete ran behind him. "I feel I should warn you that although it really wasn't me who clocked you the first time, I'm getting the strangest urges right this minute."

Jonathan ignored him. It was only a little after eight, and yet the village appeared to be absolutely deserted, every blind drawn and not a chink of light anywhere. Except in the pub. So maybe every inhabitant of Kiltone did gather in the pub, every night. What did their children do?

They were away from the village now, and passing the church, a small, rectangular stone building with a surprisingly high steeple, standing starkly alone, several hundred yards from the last house. Beyond was the cemetery, and then nothing but open meadow. So what does one usually associate with a full moon? Werewolves and witchcraft? Which was just ridiculous. Spring tides? Now there was something to think about.

"We won't follow her up the path," he decided. "We'll cut across that field behind the church and go straight up."

"You ever done any mountaineering?" Pete wanted to know. "I've climbed that path over there, and it's so steep it has to go up in switchbacks. What the hillside is like doesn't bear thinking about."

"So let's stop thinking about it and get on." Jonathan found his way round the graveyard. He couldn't resist a glance to his right. The headstones seemed to be alive, moving to and fro in the moonlight. Otto Benderer would be lying only a few feet away, amused at having caused all this excitement in death, making up for the immortality he had just missed in life!

Or maybe it was all the moonlight. And the Irish air. The field was rather soft, and the mud was clinging. His shoes were going to be in a mess.

"I forgot to mention," Pete said. "There are supposed to be a few bogs in this vicinity. You want to keep your eyes open."

"There wouldn't be anything dangerous so close to the village," Jonathan told him. "Anyway, here's the cliffside."

It rose above them, unpleasantly steep, but by no means impossible to climb; the turf was soft and full of rabbit holes and other footholds. Nor was it quite so high as it had appeared from the village. Jonathan went up, hand over hand, and after a moment's hesitation, Pete began to climb beneath him. Pete Rodgers, here to do a story on fox hunting. It was a possibility, of course. They did a lot of fox hunting in certain parts of the States, so far as Jonathan knew. On the other hand, there were so many bigger and more famous hunts in Eire than one run by an obviously odd British aristocrat. And Pete had arrived yesterday afternoon. There was a coincidence, if you happened to believe in such things.

Muscles aching, sweat pouring down his face, he flung a hand over the top, dug his fingers into the soft turf, and pulled himself up. He sat there, panting for some seconds, until Pete joined him.

"Brother," said the American. "When we could be sitting in a warm pub, drinking beer."

Jonathan was on his knees, peering over the bluff. It was, in fact, only one of a series of bluffs, which extended into the narrow headland sheltering the harbor. And Joan Herries, if the girl they had seen had been Joan Herries, had disappeared. But she would hardly have climbed all the way up here just to climb down again on the same side.

"Let's take a look on the other side of the point," he said.

"It's only the sea," Pete told him. "Like I said, I came up here yesterday afternoon. Felt like the exercise."

"But there's a way down on the far side?"

"Several, I should think. Steep little paths."

"And what's down there?"

"Beach. Miles and miles of beach. Shingle, mostly, though. Not much good for swimming."

"What time did you make your trip?"

"Oh, say four-thirty. Why, is it important?"

"Four hours earlier, yesterday. And there were miles and miles of beach. Come on, Pete me lad." He got up and began walking quickly toward the seaward side of the headland.

"You mean you're interested in the tides?" Pete asked. "So it'll be about half tide up now. There won't be too much beach around."

"There won't be any beach around in another half an hour, which is what I find interesting." Jonathan reached the far side of the first bluff, gazed out to sea. It occurred to him that this was where George Herries, or Otto Benderer, had been fond of sitting, staring out to sea and thinking, what? "Look over there."

There were several small islands, most of them hardly larger than rocks, cluttering the sea beyond the point. But beyond them, on the near horizon, perhaps two miles from the beach, a light winked.

"Well, what *do* you know," Pete said. "Smugglers, you think?"

"Could be."

"I take it you can read Morse."

"Whatever they're signaling, it's in code. I imagine they're asking if it's safe to come in."

Pete scratched his head. "And this is somehow linked with young Joan and that crack on your head? Such as how?"

"Frankly, I have no idea," Jonathan said. "I

can't see any reason for anything, right this moment. But there's a link, all right. I'm sure of that." He dropped to his hands and knees, crawled to the edge of the cliff, lay down, and looked over. The beach—or as much of it as was left, which was just a sliver of sand—lay immediately beneath him, but was in deep shadow. Yet there were people down there; he caught a glimpse of a white sweater and the flutter of a skirt. The young people of Kiltone, presumably. "They're waiting for her, all right."

"Then maybe we'd better make ourselves scarce," Pete said.

"You do that," Jonathan suggested.

"But you aim to find out what's going on, eh? Just who are you, Anders?"

"A newspaper reporter," Jonathan said. "But this could be something pretty big. Hasn't it occurred to you that the Ulster border is only twenty miles away, behind us?"

"And there's a sort of undeclared war going on all the time between the Republic and the British bit," Pete said, half to himself.

"Well, let's say that a lot of the Irish still figure that all of Ireland should be one country: theirs. And the more extremist elements in the Irish Republican Army are prepared to do something about it, from time to time."

"Yeah. Well, in my opinion they could have a point. Seems to me, before we go any further, we ought to decide which side we're on. And seeing as how you're British, I guess yours is decided for you."

"I just want to find out if it *is* guns they're meaning to smuggle," Jonathan said. "It's not a question of sides. I'm against gunrunning on principle. Sometimes they go off and people get killed."

"Yeah," Pete said thoughtfully. "There's another point. How do we get down?"

"There's a path, just over there. That's what they used."

"But they'll have a watch on that. We'll have to do our mountaineering bit again."

"I should have thought to bring my binoculars." Jonathan took another long look out to sea. The lamp had stopped winking, and he could not see the ship. Had he come along at this moment, he'd have no idea that anything was happening at all. But now, beneath them on the shore, there were two other faint glimmers of light, one on the rocks by the water's edge, the other a little way up the cliffside. The signals the smuggler had been asking for were in place, leading lights to guide him through the rocks.

"Let's get down there." Jonathan started descending. Was he doing the right thing? He was here to find out what he could about Otto Benderer, not to combat Irish extremists. On the other hand, how could he, a British agent, overlook a threat against a part of Great Britain itself? Because if there were guns in that ship, they could only be intended for Ulster. And there was always the possibility that this might be connected with Benderer, if Benderer's daughter was involved. Certainly it could do no harm to find out just what was coming ashore.

But he wished his head would stop its spinning.

A pebble landed right where he hurt most. He looked up. "Be careful," he whispered. They were going down far faster than they could ever go back up. Within only a few seconds they had reached the beach, perhaps a hundred yards to the right of the waiting party. Jonathan heard Pete land beside him and pointed to an outcrop of rock by the water's edge, considerably closer to the likely scene of action. To gain this necessitated crossing an open expanse of beach, but the moon had not reached down here, and they would only be exposed for a couple of seconds.

"Run!" he whispered, and dashed across the sand, throwing himself into the shade of a rocky outcrop. Here he was at water level, and the next wave lapped around him, soaking him most disagreeably.

"For pity's sake," Pete complained. "My glasses are all blurred. Hold on a moment." He produced a handkerchief to clean them. "I wish you'd told me we were going to go swimming at midnight."

Jonathan crawled between the rocks. He was so wet by now that a little more water hardly mattered. Each wave came rippling between the boulders, soaking his hands and feet. But the wind was onshore, and there were other sounds now as well. An engine, rumbling very faintly, and then, far more clearly, the rattle of an anchor chain, followed by silence.

He peered round the last boulder. There were six people on the beach. It was difficult to see more than that in the darkness. They had moved away from the cliff base and stood close to the water, looking out to sea. Out there was still blackness, but the waiting people stood directly in the line drawn between the two lanterns. And now a boat was approaching the shore. He could hear the creaking of the oarlocks.

"Spooky," Pete said at his elbow. "Like stepping back a couple of hundred years into history, eh?

Landing French wines and perfumes on the south coast of England. Or a spy from Napoleon, what? Don't remind me. I'm a romantic."

"So be quiet," Jonathan begged. If it *was* guns, how on earth could they get heavy crates up that narrow winding path to the surface?

"Sure now," said a voice behind them. "Ye're after getting yourselves all wet, when ye shouldn't be here at all."

They looked up at a tall, heavily built young man, whose principal feature was a large broken nose, which suggested that he might have been a prize fighter. Or perhaps that he still was. Even more disturbing than his physical appearance, however, was the shotgun he carried under his arm.

"That's it." Pete stood up. "Good evening to you."

Jonathan also stood up and made a quick estimate of their chances. But he did not like the look of them. Presumably between them they could deal with this chap, if they acted quickly enough. But they could hardly do that without alarming the other people, only a few yards away, and a quick dash up the beach promised nothing with this rising tide. He did not know if there was going to be another way up the cliff, and failing that there was every possibility that they'd be cut off and drowned.

"We'll join me friends," suggested the pugilist.

"I guess we shall," Pete said. "I kind of thought they'd have a lookout."

"So you said," Jonathan agreed. And he had accepted the idea that the lookout would be on the path. He could use his still-aching head as an excuse for such carelessness. Certainly there was no point in brooding on that now.

They splashed out of the water and across the sand to the group of people.

"What the . . . ?" asked one of the men.

"Spotted them skulking around the rocks back there," the boxer said.

"It's the two blokes from the inn," said another man.

"Mr. Rodgers? And Mr. Anders?" Joan Herries came forward. Now that they were close to the group, Jonathan saw that it consisted of four men and two girls, the eldest of whom was younger than himself.

"Guilty, I'm afraid, Joan," Pete said.

"Oh, really, Mr. Rodgers," she said. "Ye should have stayed at home."

"Believe me, I wish I had."

"So do we all," said the first young man, the one whose white seaman's sweater Jonathan had also seen from above. "Well, now ye're here . . ."

"Ye may as well meet everybody," Joan said. "This is Mick. He's our leader."

Mick was an extremely good-looking fellow, Jonathan realized.

"And this is Tim."

"Well, hello to yourself," Tim said. He was the taxi driver. Of course.

"And this is Joe," Joan went on. "And here's George. And that's Paddy." She pointed to the man with the shotgun.

"Pleased to meet you," Jonathan said, and wondered if he were dreaming.

"Charmed, I'm sure," Pete agreed.

"And what about me?" demanded the other girl, a short, plump young woman, with red hair and a pleasantly ugly face.

"And this is Pat," Joan said. "She's Paddy's twin, really, but they don't look much alike, do they?"

In fact, Jonathan thought, they could hardly look less alike.

"But what are we going to do about those fellows?" Tim wanted to know. "They'll be ashore in a minute."

"We can't stop them now," Mick decided. "There's not too much time as it is, on this tide. Ye two fellows can just give us a hand." He hesitated. "Ye wouldn't be after trying anything funny, now, would ye? Paddy's gun is loaded."

"We'll be good," Jonathan agreed.

The rowing boat was now into the shallows. Tim and Joe splashed into the water to seize the gunwales and two of the crew also jumped overboard to run it up on the beach. From the bow there stepped a bearded man in a peaked cap and a heavy sweater.

"Good evening, Mr. O'Reilly," he said, in decidedly broken English. "You have reinforcements?"

"Problems, ye mean," Mick said. "But we'll worry about that. Let's get your stuff ashore."

"Agreed. There are seven boxes."

"Come on, lads. Ye too, Mr. Anders. And ye, Mr. Rodgers."

They waded into the shallow water, unloaded the boxes, each some four feet long and two wide, and extremely heavy, so that it took two men to lift one.

Jonathan and Pete worked in harness, carrying them up the beach and well clear of the water. Although Jonathan still couldn't figure how they were going to get them up the cliff.

"So here's your money," Mick said, when the last box had been brought ashore. "And ye'll be back, when?"

"If you wish it, Mr. O'Reilly, I can be back in three weeks," said the captain. "If you wish it." He gazed at Jonathan and Pete, clearly understanding that they did not belong here.

"Oh, sure, that'll be fine, captain," Mick said. "Three weeks and the tide will be just right. We'll be here. Good night, captain, And bon voyage."

They shook hands. "Good night to you, Mr. O'Reilly. And to you all," said the captain. "And success in your struggle."

The dinghy was relaunched, and the oars creaked as it pulled into the darkness.

"Now, what nationality might he be?" Jonathan asked.

"Ye mind your own business," Paddy growled.

"And let's get these boxes into shelter," Mick said.

Tim and Joe went first, George and Mick second, and Jonathan and Pete came last, with Paddy and his shotgun immediately behind them. The two girls accompanied them, each carrying a flashlight.

They carried their loads up the beach, moving slowly on the soft sand, and right in beneath the base of the cliff itself. But they couldn't be meaning to leave them here, Jonathan thought.

They didn't. At the base of the cliff was a small

aperture, scarcely more than a hole in the rock. Here the boxes were laid on the sand, and they returned for the rest, until all seven were just outside the hole.

"What's up, d'ye think?" Pete whispered. "Surely the tide gets above here?"

"Yeah," Jonathan agreed.

"So quit your whispering and get to work," Mick commanded.

Joe and Tim had already crawled through, and the hole was just large enough to push one of the boxes behind them. This was Jonathan and Pete's job, and hard work it was too, while Paddy stood guard over them, and Mick cast anxious glances at the flooding tide, now seeping up the beach to within twenty feet of where they stood.

"Come on, now," he said, when the last box had gone through. "Ye next, George."

He didn't miss a trick, Jonathan realized. He wanted a majority of his own people on either side of the entrance.

"Now ye two," Mick commanded.

Jonathan went first, crawling through the narrow opening to discover himself, as he had expected, in a small cave with a roof perhaps eight feet high. The cave outlines were lost in the darkness, although Joe now also had a flashlight switched on. But how did they keep the water out?

Pete came through, and then the girls, and lastly Mick and Paddy.

"Now let's get a move on," Mick said.

Once again it was a case of hefting the boxes, while each of the girls once again took a lamp and led the way. And Jonathan had his question answered.

There was no chance of keeping the water out, but the boxes were being carried above high-water mark. For at the rear of this first cave there was a passageway, formed by a deep fault in the rock, which sloped gently upward. This they followed, although with every step the box grew heavier and heavier. And there was still another load to come. And he still didn't know what was in them.

After what seemed an eternity, the passage leveled off, and a few steps more brought them to another rock chamber, even larger than the first, and strikingly reminiscent of pictures Jonathan had seen of Egyptian tombs, for along the sides of the chambers the walls had been hollowed out to make large shelves. On these, perhaps three feet above the floor level of the cave, the boxes were placed. And for a very good reason, he realized; for although the shelves and the walls of the chamber were quite dry, the floor was discolored and damp, and it was clear that at spring tides the sea reached even up here.

"Come on now, hurry," Mick commanded.

They ran back down the passage to the first cave. Here Mick gave an anxious glance through the hole; the water was lapping at the sill.

Once again they hefted three boxes between them, while this time Paddy handed over his shotgun to his sister, and he and Joan themselves lifted the last box. Jonathan glanced over his shoulder at Pete, and then decided against trying anything. He wasn't sure that Pete would back him, he wasn't sure that even between them they could take on five husky Irish lads, and he wasn't sure that Pat, for all her diminutive femininity might not be capable of using the shotgun.

But he was determined to find out what was in the boxes. He followed Joe and Tim up the sloping passage until they reached the second chamber, where Pat was waiting with her flashlight. Then he stumbled, gave an exclamation of disgust, and let his hands slip from the iron handle.

The box hit the rock with a crash, and obligingly split, but not sufficiently for him to see inside.

"Now that wasn't at all nice, Mr. Anders," Mick panted, hefting his own box onto its shelf.

"I guess the lid was supposed to fly off," Pete said. "It always does in the movies."

"Movies," Joan said disgustedly. "Now really, Mr. Anders, ye're not being very cooperative."

"And why should he be?" Tim demanded. "Didn't I tell ye, he's no newspaperman. He's a police spy, he is. Or worse. Why d'ye think he's here tonight?"

"Was it you batted me one?" Jonathan asked.

"Sure, well, I'm sorry about that, Mr. Anders. I didn't expect ye back so soon. Joan told me ye were taking a tub."

Jonathan looked at Joan.

"Well," she said. "I could tell ye weren't a reporter. Ye just didn't look like one. Man, we've had so many reporters around here this last week I can smell them."

"And Pete here qualifies?"

"I thought so. Up to now."

"Believe me," Pete said. "I only wish I knew what was going on. I came along with Anders just to make sure he behaved himself. He sure lit out after you with a mean look in his eye."

"And leaving me dinner to spoil?" Joan demanded.

"Well, after all, you were responsible for this bump on my head," Jonathan pointed out.

"When ye're all finished gabbling," Mick said, "perhaps ye'd like to tell us just who ye are, Mr. Anders. We could do with a little bit of truth."

"I'm a newspaper reporter," Jonathan explained patiently. "Come to do a piece on Joan's mother. Sorry I don't look like one, Joan. We're cultivating a new breed."

"Sure and he's a great liar," Tim said.

"Well, it's no matter," Mick said. "No matter for either of them, the more's the pity. They're here and they shouldn't be here. And that's a fact."

"Sure now," the girl called Pat said. "Ye'll not be doing any violence to these two nice young men."

"Ye don't seem to understand," Mick explained. "We are fighting a war. So if the other side don't care to get the message, that's their bad luck. But if these two go away from here, with what they've seen, it'll likely mean prison for the lot of us. And we won't be able to use this way in for the guns again. And so I figure we'll have to be hard."

"Ye can't," Joan cried.

"We have no choice. But ye'll have a vote, now. Those in favor of letting them go, speak up."

Joan raised her hand, and after a moment's hesitation, Pat followed her example. The men exchanged glances.

"Well now," Mick said. "Those in favor of seeing they don't ever tell what they saw here?"

All the men raised their hands.

"So there ye are," Mick said. "I'm sorry, gentlemen, and if there was any other way, I'd take ye down to the pub meself and buy ye each a pint. But as there isn't, I figure I have to inform ye that ye have just been condemned to death."

CHAPTER 3

"I can't say I think very much of your sense of humor," Pete Rodgers remarked.

"It's not a joke, Mr. Rodgers," Mick protested. "We have to protect ourselves. And the Army."

"My dear fellow, you can't go around condemning people to death, just like that. Can they, Jonathan?"

Jonathan said nothing. He had an uneasy feeling that they could, and just had.

"And without a trial and all," Joan declared. "Just a show of hands. That's not Christian."

"Is it a trial ye're after?" Tim demanded. "So what would ye say in their defense? Sure and they're foreign agents, all right, or they'd admit it, wouldn't they?"

Which was an entirely Irish piece of reasoning Jonathan could not fathom at all.

"And ye yourself know he's not a newspaperman," George put in. "It was ye who told us. So what else can he be?"

"But ye're taking too much upon yourselves." Pat gazed defiantly at her brother. "Ye too, Paddy. Ye don't have the authority, Mick. I say we must telephone Sligo."

"Now, how can we use the telephone for a matter like this?" Mick asked.

"Tim has the car," Joan argued. "And Pat is right. This is a matter for them big fellows to decide."

Mick glanced at his friends.

"Maybe the girls are right," Joe muttered. " 'Tis a mighty big thing, to take a life. And ye did not specify who was going to do it."

"A mighty big thing," Paddy said.

"All right," Mick said. "All right. So we take a ride into Sligo. With these two chaps?"

"Leave them here," Joan suggested. "They'll be safe enough down here. Ye can bind them up."

"Oh, thanks very much," Pete said.

Jonathan listened, and waited, and wondered. They were a very odd bunch, not really killers, not even true extremists, he felt; their attitude was that of taking part in a vast game. He thought that a great deal might be going to happen in the near future. He even thought that, given time, these chaps might be very useful. He did not like the idea of their taking the whole matter to some battle-scarred and hate-filled I.R.A. commander in Sligo.

"Say, now, that's a good idea," Tim said. "We'll tie them up and leave them right here. This isn't one of the highest tides, so it'll no more than about cover the floor. And no one but us even knows these caves exist."

"But we'll leave a guard, nonetheless," Mick decided. "Paddy, ye're elected."

"To stay here all the night?" the ex-boxer demanded. "All by meself?"

"Ye have the shotgun."

"And ye won't be by yourself, ye great lummox; ye'll have the two gentlemen to keep ye company," Joe pointed out.

"And it won't be for all night," George added. "We'll be back inside of three hours."

"Ah, it isn't at all necessary to leave poor Paddy," Joan said. "Who's going to find his way down here?"

"Paddy's staying, and that's final," Mick said. "So let's get the two gentlemen bound up and be on our way."

With great enthusiasm they set to tying Pete's and Jonathan's hands behind their backs, and then their ankles together, seating them against the wall.

"There," Mick said. "Ye're not too uncomfortable, I hope, Mr. Anders?"

"Not too," Jonathan agreed.

"Well, there'll be a bit of water in here in a little while, but it won't cause ye any trouble, I should not think, seeing that ye're all wet already. And we'll be back as quick as we can. We don't want ye sitting there in the damp all night."

"I'm sure you don't," Pete agreed. "You don't think it would be cheaper to let us die of pneumonia? Think of the saving in bullets. Ah, well, may I wish you five punctures?"

"Oh, he's a wit, he is," Ted said. "Ye all right, Paddy?"

"Give me that other flashlight. Ye'll only need the one." Paddy sat on a vacant shelf opposite Pete and Jonathan, a flashlight on either side of him, the shotgun across his knees. "I'm all right. Now."

"Well, so long," Mick said. "Come along, girls."

Pat looked as if she was about to make a final protest, but then she looked at Joan and instead shrugged. They left by the upper opening, obviously following another of the sloping passageways which in time must lead to the surface, Jonathan presumed. He wondered if man had played any part in hollowing out such a honeycomb; it seemed likely, as this was a smuggler's paradise.

"Here's a pretty kettle of fish," Pete remarked. "Or cave of fish, I should say. I say, old man, are you really a reporter? Or what these characters think you are?"

"Whatever I am," Jonathan said, "I'm really not here to look out for gun smugglers, and if Tim hadn't hit me I'd be home in bed right this minute. That's the truth, Paddy. I came to interview Mrs. Herries, and if you must know, to find out what the Russians are doing in Kiltone. Our editor has a suspicion of Russians."

"Haven't we all," Pete agreed. "So what do you say, Paddy? Suppose we gave you a solemn promise not to say a word about tonight, will you let us go?"

"That I will not," Paddy said. "I've had me orders and that's final. So I'd suggest ye be quiet."

"It's going to be difficult," Pete said. "You hear what I hear, Jonathan?"

The ripple of water came seeping up the lower

passage, not visible in the darkness, but louder than it should have been because the cave was itself acting as a natural amplifier.

"It's going to be damp, all right," Jonathan agreed.

"Well, ye'll just have to grin and bear it," Paddy pointed out. "No one asked ye to come following Joan, anyway. It's not decent. As for the dent in your skull, maybe Tim should have hit ye a bit harder right then, and we wouldn't have had all this trouble."

"I love you, too," Jonathan said.

"Here it comes," Pete said. The flashlights were shining directly on them, but enough of a glare was thrown sideways to reach the entrance to each of the two tunnels, and into the lower opening there came the first of the water, lapping over the cavern floor, trickling up to where the two men sat.

"Wasn't this a method of execution once upon a while?" Pete asked.

"In Scotland, I think," Jonathan said. "They tied witches to a stake where the tide would just cover their heads. A kind of trial by ordeal. If they weren't drowned, they were innocent."

"Maybe it was used in Ireland as well," Pete suggested.

"Ah, quit worrying," Paddy said. "It'll not come in more than an inch or two."

"It's already an inch or two," Jonathan told him. "And decidedly cold. I hope you fellows worked out your tides right."

"It'll be the top of the flood now," Paddy said. "Sure, in another half an hour it'll be taking off again. What's that?"

From the corridor to their left there came a stealthy rustling.

"Maybe the water's coming in from that way as well," Pete said. "You fellows want to know something hysterical? I don't like our situation very much."

"That's not water." Paddy got up, took his shotgun in one hand and his flashlight in the other, and walked to the upper entrance, splashing through the shallow water. "I never knew they had rats down here."

"I don't think he likes our situation much either," Jonathan whispered.

"At least he's left the other light," Pete said. "If he gets scared he's just as likely to take off and leave us alone. In the dark."

Again there came the long scraping sound from the darkness beyond the entrance.

"That's no rat," Jonathan said.

"Aye," Paddy agreed, half to himself. "Who's there?" he called, directing the beam of the flashlight into the aperture. His voice held a distinct quaver.

"Maybe it's one of the little people," Jonathan suggested.

"Ah, shut your gob." Paddy went into the passageway, and they lost sight of him, although they could still see the glimmer of the flashlight. "Who is it? Stop your games, now. I've me shotgun here, and I'll blast your head off."

The scraping continued.

"Someone digging?" Pete asked.

Jonathan did not reply. He thought it sounded

more like someone dragging something over the ground.

"I see ye," Paddy shouted from farther away than he had seemed to be. "I see ye. Stop, damn ye."

Now there was a whole series of sounds from inside the tunnel, the original rustling, the stamping of Paddy's feet, and then the rest was drowned in a most tremendous explosion as he fired his shotgun. The entire cliff seemed to jump, and Jonathan could have sworn the rock wall against which he leaned moved.

"Wow," Pete gasped. "I hope he doesn't do that too often or we really are going to be stuck in here."

Jonathan watched the inner entrance. There was another sound now, closer at hand, and a moment later Joan came in. "Sssh, now," she said. "We've only a second."

"But how on earth . . ." Pete wanted to know.

"Sssh." She knelt beside him, took a knife from the pocket of her jacket and cut his bonds. A moment later Jonathan was also free. "Now let's get out of here," she whispered, "before Paddy comes back."

She led them into the upper passageway. Here it was pitch dark, but a sudden glimmer of light from some distance in front of them warned them that Paddy was indeed on his way back.

"Hold my hand," she whispered. "And Mr. Anders, ye take Mr. Rodgers' hand."

Jonathan obeyed and followed Pete into a side tunnel leading off to the right. Here the darkness was so intense he could not even see Pete, who was only an arm's length in front of him.

And now there was another explosion of sound. "Oh, where have ye gone?" Paddy bellowed. "Come back, ye silly men. Get lost in these passages and ye'll be here forever."

Joan never hesitated for an instant. The passage twisted and turned, and steadily climbed; once they even brushed by another opening, but Joan seemed to know exactly where she was going.

"Now we have to crawl," she said at last. "But it's only a short distance."

They dropped to their hands and knees. Jonathan put one hand above his head, and sure enough, the ceiling of the passage was only just above him. If it came any lower they'd have to wriggle. But it didn't, and a few minutes later Joan was parting some bushes to allow a shaft of brilliant moonlight to enter the aperture.

They crawled onto the hilltop, a good hundred yards from the cliff edge. "Don't stand up," Joan said. "Not yet." She stuck two fingers into her mouth and gave a shrill whistle, which was promptly answered from a few yards away; and a moment later a dark shadow detached itself from a clump of bushes and ran toward them.

"Pat?" Jonathan asked. "But Paddy . . . ?"

"Is me own brother. And he actually took a shot at me, the crazy man. He's a right tearaway."

"Well, Pete said. "I sure am glad to see you two girls. Now let's get out of here."

"Not so fast," Joan said. "We have to let Paddy work off his trouble first. Oh, he's no fool. He'll know ye have to come out on the cliffside, somewhere."

"He doesn't know about this entrance?" Jonathan asked.

"He only knows about the one," she said scornfully. "And he'll be scared to try the others. Heck, I showed them that cave in the first place. I was born in Kiltone and wandered all over these cliffs with me father, when I was just a child. He'd explored every inch of those passageways, and there's no one alive now knows them like I do."

"There he is," Pat said. "Ah, there'll be no living with him for the rest of the week. He'll be just wild, he will."

Paddy stood on the hillside, perhaps two hundred yards away, a large dark shadow, glaring this way and that, the shotgun cocked and the flashlight hanging from his wrist.

"He'll figure he ought to see ye in the moonlight," Joan explained. "And he will, too, if ye don't stay down."

They crouched by the bushes and waited while Paddy walked up and down, and then suddenly turned and went back inside.

"We'll wait a while," Pat said. "He's a sly one, he is."

And sure enough, a few moments later Paddy re-emerged to make another inspection of the empty hillside. Following which he again returned inside.

"It'll be all right now," Pat said. "He'll have gone back to the guns to wait for Mick. Oh, he's going to be furious."

"Well, we'd best get on our way before the others

come back," Joan said. "Ye'll have to walk awhile, Mr. Rodgers, and ye as well, Mr. Anders. But the only taxi around here belongs to Tim. Ye walk inland to the next village, it's not more than five miles, and ye'll find a car there."

"Not a chance," Jonathan said. "We're not going anywhere. I'm not, anyway."

"Ye don't seem to understand." Joan led them down the hillside. "Those boys weren't fooling. They'd have done ye down, all right. They just have no sense of perspective when it involves the Army."

"But you two are members of the Army, too," Pete said.

"Well, so we are, Mr. Rodgers. But I'm against killing."

"And won't you be in trouble when they find out about tonight?"

"Who's to tell them?" Pat asked.

"Mind ye," Joan said. "We'd take it kindly if ye'll promise not to say a word about tonight's happening, but just pack your things and leave Kiltone."

"That seems an entirely reasonable point of view to me," Pete said. "Don't you agree, Jonathan?"

"No, I don't," Jonathan said. "I came here to do a job, and I'm certainly not going to be chased off by a bunch of Irish terrorists."

"So I'm a terrorist, now," Joan declared. "There's gratitude for ye."

"I didn't mean you," Jonathan explained. "But …"

"But nothing," Pete said. "I think you're taking quite the wrong attitude, Jonathan." By now they had regained the outskirts of the village. "If you keep up that point of view, these two young ladies might hand us back to their friends."

"Say, there's an idea," Pat said. "We should've left them there, Joannie."

"I thought they were different," Joan admitted. "Well, I *knew* Mr. Rodgers was different."

"Then why not try calling me Pete," Pete suggested. "Seeing as how we're going to be friends."

"Are we?" Joan asked doubtfully.

"Now listen," Jonathan said. "When the pair of you are finished billing and cooing . . ."

"Just don't get excited, Jonathan, old man," Pete said. "We're going to do like the little lady says, and be grateful to her for giving us the chance. So come on."

"Just who do you think you are?" Jonathan demanded.

"If you'll give me half a moment, I'll tell you. You girls go and have a pint apiece, and give us five minutes to get changed and collect our things, and we'll be off."

He half pushed Jonathan into the doorway of the inn.

"Now you just look here," Jonathan said.

"Sssh." Pete ran up the stairs, and after a moment's hesitation, Jonathan followed. He certainly wanted to change; he was both cold and wet. And after everything that had happened it was not yet midnight. The bar was still full and very active; the piper had started playing again. The two girls went in and were greeted with a chorus of cheers.

Pete was waiting on the landing. "Now nip along

to your room and get changed, and we'll hightail it out of here."

"You were going to give me a reason. Maybe you've forgotten that those characters landed a half brick or whatever on the back of my head. I'm not likely to forget that."

"And in addition, your British hackles are rising at the idea of them gaily smuggling guns into the country for use against your people in Ulster. Well, you have a point. But neither of us is likely to accomplish very much of what we came for if we have to spend our time fending off the I.R.A."

"And what *did* we come for?" Jonathan asked.

"Well, for starters, you're no more a reporter than I'm the man in the moon."

"And you're not the man in the moon?"

"Listen," Pete said. "I have an idea we're both working in the same direction, and if we don't cooperate, we're justly likely to mess each other up. I'm C.I.A."

"Glad to have you aboard. I was beginning to get that general idea."

"And you're B.S.S. Right?"

"Every time. And what are you after?"

"Finding out what our Red friends are doing in Kiltone. And you?"

"Partly the same thing. But we're also interested in whether old Benderer did leave anything worth having."

"Joan's father," Pete muttered. "And she's one sweet kid. It's a rugged world."

"She's not involved. I hope. Except with the I.R.A. trigger-happies."

"But you're going to forget all about them."

"I'll have to brood on that. Because I'm also brooding on something else. Suppose Old Otto did leave something behind. He used to go sit on those cliffs every day. Right over that network of caves. And Joan says she knows every inch of them, and she's the only one around here who does."

"Say, you might just have something there. But first things first. We can't go back down those caves until her boyfriends have given us up and gone home. And we don't even want to be in the village when they come back from Sligo. So I say we go along with the girls and push off. Or appear to push off."

"And go where? That's a mighty blank-looking countryside out there. You're not seriously thinking of walking five miles to the next village?"

"As a matter of fact, no. I'm thinking that there's a nice big castle with a few dozen empty rooms just up the hill from here."

"And a few Russians, as well."

"Company is fun, don't you think?

"And our appearance won't scare them off, or something?"

"I've been brooding on a way to get amongst them ever since I got here. That's why I put out the fox hunting bit, although in any event I wasn't keen on going in there all on my lonesome. But two of us, one American and the other British, why, it's far more likely that we'd be reporters than security people. So our car broke down on our way into Kiltone."

"It's an idea. And we've both come to cover the fox hunting?"

"Why not? So get packing."

It was a pretty crazy world, Jonathan decided. But Pete did have a point. Hanging around here *was* going to be difficult with Mick and his friends on the rampage. And under the circumstances, he was rather glad to have accumulated a bit of help. Supposing that Pete was everything he claimed to be.

He changed his clothes, wrapped his wet things in his dressing gown and crammed them into the suitcase. Closing it, he returned to the landing where Pete was waiting for him, also carrying a case as well as an outsize camera.

"I wonder if the girls will be around to say goodby," the American said wistfully.

"Well, we can't afford to hang about. Come on."

They tiptoed down the stairs and through the lobby into the street.

"Pssst!" Joan and Pat stood by the front door.

"We were kind of keeping a watch," Pat explained. "They haven't come back yet, but it's not going to be very long now. So be careful, do."

"We will be," Jonathan promised. "What about you two?"

"Sure and we'll be off to bed," Joan said. "Well, that's what they told us to do, isn't it? Go to bed and forget all about tonight, Mick said. And forget all about those two fellows, too."

"Well, I want you to know that I'm very grateful, Joan," Jonathan said. "And to you, Pat. And I wasn't after your smuggling friends, honest."

"Sure and I'm sorry ye had to take a knock on the head, Mr. Anders. But we can't afford to take risks."

As if she weren't taking a few herself right this minute.

"Anyway, we're certainly going to forget all about it," Pete assured her. "But not about you two."

"Sure and ye're a fellow to remember yourself," Joan said. "Take care." She went inside, and Pat hurried up the street to her home.

Pete sighed. "When this little lot is over, I might just come back down to this inn. You know that girl *can* cook?"

"When this little lot is over," Jonathan reminded him. "Business before pleasure."

"On the other hand," he remembered, after they'd been walking for half an hour, "I didn't have any dinner." His head was opening and closing with every step.

"I told you you'd made a mistake. Whew! Let's rest a while."

They sat on their suitcases. Although it was well past midnight, the moon still hung in the sky like a gigantic electric bulb, and the coastline was depicted as if it were a relief map. Jonathan figured they were about halfway up the hill; below them the village of Kiltone huddled darkly about its tiny harbor, and in the background the bluffs rose sharply from the water's edge. He wondered if Paddy was still grimly seated in the cavern, shotgun across his knees, brooding on their whereabouts.

But their interest was in what lay ahead. They could see the castle now, foursquare in the moonlight, a black box dominating the hills above them.

"Quiet, isn't it?" Pete remarked.

"Not now," Jonathan pointed out. "Let's dive."

The throbbing of the car engine filled the night, and they could see the headlights flaring over the next shallow rise. They threw themselves flat on the ground on the slight downward slope beside the road, suitcases tucked in against their bodies. But they were not in much danger of being spotted, Jonathan decided; the car was traveling much too fast. It zoomed past them and disappeared over the next rise.

"Think it was our friends?" Pete asked.

"Could hardly be anyone else."

"So let's see; they'll be at the bottom of the cliffs in five minutes. They'll have to walk from there, and then it'll be another half an hour before they find we're gone. Say, that's not too much time."

"So let's rush. But we'll stick to the road for as long as we can. Remember what you were telling me about bogs?"

"Yeah, man," Pete said.

They walked up the road; the castle loomed ever larger on their left. Half an hour later they had reached the gates, enormous stone pillars, surmounted by an equally outsize lintel on which there was a crest, a double-headed cat crouching over what might have been a field mouse.

"Fantastic," Pete said. "But these things look locked to me. Would you believe it? Locked gates with no wall. I guess that's what you'd expect, seeing as how we're in Ireland."

"It's just to keep cars out, I'd say," Jonathan suggested. "Let's get on."

They followed the enormous pillars down a slight slope, tramped through some soft ground, came up on the farther side, and found themselves on a metaled drive. The castle was directly in front of them.

"Well, what do you know," Jonathan remarked. "It really is only the one building. I thought it was an optical illusion."

"Just a keep," Pete said. "Norman, I figure. They didn't build all that many of those great motte and bailey things. A big tower like this one, garrison for say twenty or thirty men at arms, was usually sufficient to keep down sparsely populated areas." He glanced at Jonathan. "History is my hobby. One of the reasons I enjoy being posted in Ireland. This place just drips history."

"What worries me is if they'll have room for us, after all," Jonathan said.

"Oh, you'll find it's bigger inside than it looks," Pete assured him.

They arrived before the drawbridge, which spanned a ditch—it could hardly be called a moat, although it was some twelve feet deep and another six wide; the bottom was a green scum. But the bridge itself was fixed, a good eight feet broad, and led to an iron-studded gate.

"Quite impressive," Pete said. "Of course, that wood isn't the original, and the stonework has all been redone, fairly recently, I'd say. But with considerable taste. It's been rebuilt exactly as it must have been in twelve hundred or whatever."

"Let's hope it's a bit more welcoming on the inside." Jonathan rang the bell. This at least was a modern push-button type.

"And let's hope it works," Pete said. "I can't hear it ringing."

"It works, all right," Jonathan said. "Listen to that."

From beyond the gate there began a tremendous baying and howling.

"His lordship's famous pack," Pete said.

"Here's hoping they're tied up. Somebody's coming."

There was a scraping sound inside the door, and a Judas window, set high in the oak panel, slowly opened. "What do you want?" a man asked.

Jonathan was strongly tempted to say, "A lodging for the night, if it please your lordship," or some such thing. But he decided to leave the talking to Pete, Americans being more popular in Eire than Englishmen, as a rule.

"Well, the fact is, our car has broken down, and we're looking for some help."

The man on the other side of the door gazed at them for a few moments. At last he said, "Wait a moment." More bolts scraped and the door swung slowly inward. The man on the inside was tall and thin, his face equally so, and he wore a dressing gown and slippers. But there was electric light. And that modernity, and a due regard for comfort, had been carried a stage further—a blast of heat came through the door. "What sort of help?"

"Well," Pete said, "if we could use the telephone, perhaps?"

"There is no telephone," the man said. "His lordship does not like the telephone."

"Say, mind if we have a look?" Pete asked, and darted past the butler before he could be stopped. "Yeah, man, this is really something." He stood in an enormous vaulted chamber with a stone floor, presently used as a garage and stable, and extending the full width and depth of the castle. In each corner spiral staircases mounted the tower walls, and also descended, presumably into the dungeons; the two nearest to the gate were carpeted, and obviously used by the family itself. The dogs, some twenty in number, were confined in a large pen in the far right-hand corner. Having somewhat quietened when the butler had arrived, they now recommenced barking as Pete approached; and in turn started the horses, a dozen of which were stabled in the other corner, stamping and neighing. Only the two cars, one a black Rolls and the other a small red two-seater sports model, which occupied the very center of the floor, spoiled the illusion of having stepped back in time several hundred years. "Really something," Pete shouted above the cacophony.

"Now look here," bawled the butler. "You can't come barging in here like this. This is a private residence. I've told you, I'm very sorry, but there is no telephone at Kiltone Castle. What I suggest you do is walk down the hill and you'll come to Kiltone Village. It's not far, hardly over a mile. There you'll be able to ring from the public house. You'll even be able to get a bed for the night, I should think. Ask for Mrs. Herries."

"There's a true Irish welcome for you," Pete complained. "Eh, Jonathan?"

"I have the honor to be English," the butler pointed out frigidly.

"That's even worse," Pete said. "My friend here is English. And as it happens, we're in Kiltone to cover Lord Wantage's hunt."

"My dear sir," the butler said. "I am sure that his lordship would hate the idea of being, ah, covered. He lives in Eire entirely with the idea of avoiding the public eye."

"What is all this noise about, Clay?" asked a girl's voice. "And for heaven's sake shut up those beastly dogs."

Pete and Jonathan both turned. She stood on the right-hand front staircase, a tall young woman in a crimson dressing gown. She was very blonde, with long straight hair and the most perfectly shaped features Jonathan had seen in a long while. He thought the rest of her might be just as good-looking, and figured she was a year or two younger than himself.

Pete also seemed to find her attractive. "Well, hello," he said. "Lady Wantage?"

She came down the remainder of the steps. "My mother is dead," she said. "I am Dorinda Wantage, as it happens."

"The *Honorable* Dorinda Wantage," Clay the butler pointed out.

"Pleased to meet you." Pete hurried forward behind his outstretched hand, and Dorinda Wantage took it, for a moment, before going past him to the dogs' cage.

"Sssh," she said. "Be quiet. All of you."

Their barks dwindled away, and their tails

75

drooped between their legs. The horses stopped stamping, and the silence was almost deafening.

"You sure have their number," Pete said.

She turned to face them again. "You're an American," she accused.

"Guilty as charged. My name is Pete Rodgers, and this is my friend, Jonathan Anders. He's English. We've come to Kiltone to do a piece on his lordship's hunt. Well, we didn't really mean to barge in here like this..."

"At two o'clock in the morning," Dorinda Wantage remarked.

"At two in the morning," Pete agreed. "But the fact is, our car broke down over the hill back there, and we had to hoof it. Your man suggested we go into the village. Says it's not far..."

"You came to do an article on my father's hunt? Why?"

"Well, we sort of thought it'd be interesting. Actually, I represent *Life* magazine. Maybe you've heard of it."

"Of course I've heard of *Life* magazine. And this other gentleman?"

"Jonathan Anders," Jonathan reminded her. And decided he might as well attempt to equal Pete. "I'm from *Town and Country*."

"*Are* you? How very interesting. I'm sure we can find you a room for the night."

"I do not think his lordship will care for the publicity, Miss Dorinda," Clay said.

"Oh nonsense, Clay, Papa will be tickled pink." She frowned, and peered at Jonathan. "Was there an accident?"

"Well, we sort of skidded," Pete explained. "About a mile back, like I said. And Jon sort of fell forward and bumped his head."

"He was facing the back of the car?" Dorinda Wantage asked politely.

"Eh?"

"Miss Wantage means that my bruise is on the back of my head," Jonathan said. "As a matter of fact, Miss Wantage, Pete was driving far too fast, and when he lost the road, the car turned right over."

"Good heavens," said Dorinda Wantage. "It must be a total wreck."

"That's one way of putting it. Frankly, it's just about disintegrated. I always said Pete was a reckless driver."

"Well, thank you, John Bull," Pete said.

"I think you're very lucky to be alive," Dorinda said. "And the sooner you get to bed, the better. Are those all your things? Then if you'd like to come upstairs." She led the way.

"I must tell you, Miss Wantage, this is a spectacular place," Pete said.

He certainly had a way with the ladies, Jonathan reflected somewhat ruefully.

"It is nice, isn't it? Papa has restored it exactly as it was. Of course, we had to add things like the heating and some decent furniture. But the building itself is absolutely authentic." She emerged onto the next floor, and showed them in to a comfortably furnished sitting room, off which a corridor led between a double row of doors. "This used to be the guard room and the barracks of the ordinary soldiers. We've converted it into bedrooms, back there. I'm afraid we have guests staying with us already, but there is one spare room down here, which you can have."

"That will be fine," Pete said. "Don't you agree, Jonathan, old man?"

"Oh, super," Jonathan said.

"Well then, leave your bags. Clay will put them inside for you. Would you like to see the rest of the place before you turn in?"

"We'd like that very much," Pete said. "I suppose there's no chance of a little snack? Poor old Jonathan here managed to miss dinner."

"Oh, I'm all right," Jonathan lied.

"Nonsense," Dorinda said. "Of course you must be hungry." She leaned over the banister. "Clay? Are you still there, Clay? Prepare some sandwiches and a hot drink for these gentlemen, will you?"

"Right away, Miss Dorinda," Clay said, without a great deal of pleasure.

On she went, up flight after flight, at the top of which she opened a door to admit a distinctly chilly blast of air. "Brrr. It is cold, isn't it? I mean for October. Now, this is the roof."

Jonathan walked across the slight slope to the battlements, looked out at the rolling downs below, a small wood on the other side of the road, and far away to the left, the village of Kiltone, with its sheltering bluff beyond. Was he dreaming, or did he see lights flashing out there? But up here he was safe, and did he need to feel safe right this moment. His head was more painful, and he was more exhausted than he was willing to admit, even to himself. Dorinda and Pete stood beside him.

"From here, of course," Dorinda said, "they used to defend the castle, pouring boiling oil and all that sort of thing down on the people below. Vikings, and savages, and what have you."

"Couldn't have been Vikings," Pete said. "The Normans came after the Vikings. What I mean is, they were Vikings themselves, you see, but those which had sort of settled."

"How interesting. Do you know I never knew that? You and I must have a talk, Mr. Rodgers."

"Oh, call me Pete," Pete said.

"Pete? I suppose that's short for Peter. Pete is very American. Irish, too, I suppose you could say. Would you mind terribly if I stuck to Peter? But I'd like to know more about the past. Do you know a *lot* about history?"

"Pete knows a lot about everything," Jonathan said. "I hate to rush you, Miss Wantage, but Pete was telling the truth when he said I had to miss dinner, and we've done a lot of walking since then . . ."

"And your head must be hurting like anything. How thoughtless of me. Clay will have your supper ready by now." She led them back down to the dining room, where Clay was laying out a vast plate of sandwiches and two steaming mugs of cocoa.

"My, that looks good," Pete said. "Do you mind, Dorinda?"

"It's there to be eaten."

Jonathan sat down, and hastily stood up again as one of the bedroom doors opened and another woman emerged. He felt every muscle in his body stiffening as he stared at her, and as she in turn stared at him, while her mouth slowly widened into a smile.

It was a peculiarly magnetic face, although it could hardly be described as beautiful. He had always thought her attractiveness lay in her eyes, for her features were rather sharp. But her eyes, a soft gray with a peculiar undertone of firmness, were irresistible. When she looked at you, you looked back, and became aware of your inferiority. She wore a green dressing gown and was short and slender. Her hair was an intensely fine black, cut short but not styled in any way. She was a woman once seen, never to be forgotten.

Nor, apparently, had Anna Cantelna forgotten Jonathan Anders.

"Why, Jonathan," she said. "How absolutely wonderful to meet you again."

CHAPTER 4

"You mean you know this woman?" Pete cried.

"Oh, indeed," Anna Cantelna said. "Jonathan and I are the oldest of friends. Why do you look so surprised to see me, Jonathan? I know that, thanks to you, I can never revisit England, but fortunately your government's ruling does not extend to this happy country, where I can come and go as I please."

"Good heavens," said Dorinda Wantage. "You don't mean he isn't really a reporter from *Town and Country*, Anna?"

"Is *that* what he claimed to be?" Anna smiled and came forward to stand by the table. "Oh, no, no, Dorinda. Jonathan is an agent working for the British Security Services. And this young man?"

"Pete Rodgers," Pete said. "I'm from *Life* magazine. Perhaps you've heard of it."

"I have indeed. My name is Anna Cantelna. I am a scientist. Perhaps *you* have heard of *me*. And now, perhaps, you will also tell us the truth about yourself."

"Believe me, Madam Cantelna," Pete protested. "I *have* heard of you. Oh, yes, indeed. You won the Nobel Prize a few years back for your work in marine biology. I wouldn't lie to you, Madame Cantelna. Why, do you mean to tell me that Anders here is really one of those secret agent characters? Then he's been lying to me, too."

Jonathan sat down and ate a sandwich; he was extremely hungry and needed a moment to pull his thoughts together.

"Suppose you tell us, Jonathan," Anna Cantelna invited.

"He's a reporter, all right," he said. "I was just using him; when he told me he was coming here to cover the hunting, I thought all the stars in the sky were falling into my pocket. Apologies, old man."

"*Well,*" Pete said.

"And have you nothing to say to me, Jonathan?" Anna Cantelna asked.

"You're looking very fit. As usual. What brings you to Kiltone?"

"Why, the fox hunting. Did you not understand? Dicky Wantage is an old friend of my old university professor. Dicky and I met when he was in the Soviet Union a few years ago, and he invited me to visit him whenever I had the time. So I decided to come for the hunting season. Fox hunting is one of those odd pastimes I have always wanted to try. I believe that one should sample the relaxations of all cultures. Don't you?"

Jonathan started on a second sandwich; he was beginning to feel better. "And what about your three friends?"

"Good heavens, what a lot you know about me, as usual. They are, as you say, three friends, Jonathan. Now tell us what brings *you* to Kiltone. Or needn't I ask?"

"Why you, of course," Jonathan said. "Mr. Craufurd said, go keep an eye on your old friend Anna."

Oh, that blighter. He had to have known Anna was here. So he picked Jonathan Anders. Not because this was a nice soft job which no one could mess up, but because Anna would recognize her old adversary from Guernsey and Scotland, and maybe get pushed or panicked into showing her hand. So Jonathan was nothing more than a piece of cheese stuffed into a trap. Oh, that old *blighter*!

"Do you believe him, Anna?" Dorinda asked.

"Of course, my dear child. Of course. Jonathan wouldn't lie to his old friend Anna. And as you are here, Jonathan, with *your* friend Mr. Rodgers, who has come to cover the hunt, you must ride with us tomorrow morning."

"Eh?" Jonathan asked.

"Say again?" Pete asked.

"Well, that is what you are here for," Anna pointed out. "How can you write convincingly about fox hunting, Mr. Rodgers, if you have never taken part in a meet?"

"But I don't ride horses," Pete said.

"I'm sure Dorinda will be able to find you a docile mount. And how will you, Jonathan, be able to report to Mr. Craufurd that I am really here for the hunting if you do not actually see me riding to hounds?"

"I'm afraid I don't ride either," Jonathan said.

"We have two docile mounts," Dorinda said. "Well, reasonably."

"Under the circumstances," Pete said, "I think Jonathan and I *will* go down to the village for the night. Mrs. Herries, is it?"

"Dorinda, darling," Anna said. "Would you inform Clay that these two gentlemen are staying the night?"

"I had already formed that impression, Madame Cantelna," Clay said from the top of the stairs. "If you will accompany me, gentlemen, I will show you to your room."

"Well, as the man remarked at Bastogne, nuts," Pete said. "I'll say good-by, Madame Cantelna. It's been a lot of fun, and I'm sure we'll meet again, because I'm going to be around." He went to the top of the stairs. "You going to try to stop me, Clay?"

"His lordship hates disturbances, Mr. Rodgers." Clay stepped aside.

"Wait for me," Jonathan said, hastily swallowing a third sandwich. "Bye-bye, Anna. It really has been a pleasure, believe me, but I'd rather keep an eye on you from a distance. I'm sure neither the Kremlin nor Mr. Craufurd would really like the idea of us spending the night under the same roof."

"Good-by, Jonathan," Anna said. "Or rather, good night. I'll see you in the morning. Oh, dear, Dorinda, I suppose neither of them has packed a red jacket."

"We'll find something for them to wear," Dorinda promised.

"Let's get out of here before she wakes her friends." Pete ran down the stairs.

Jonathan followed more slowly. "I'm afraid she may already have; Anna doesn't miss a trick."

But the landing was empty, although their suitcases had disappeared.

"We'll worry about them later," Pete decided, and checked on the next flight of stairs. "What on earth is that?"

There was a long growl, issuing from twenty throats and coming from the foot of the steps.

"Oh my, Clay must have let the dogs out," Dorinda said from above them. "But you don't have to worry, Peter, really. They're trained never to set foot on the carpet, so they won't venture up to you."

"And what are they likely to do if we venture down to them?"

"Well, I'm afraid I really don't know," she admitted. "They're charming, friendly creatures as a rule, toward people they like, anyway. But the trouble is, they've been starved for the last few days, except for one meal of meat. It's to make them really keen on the hunt, you know. Have you ever seen the end of a hunt, Mr. Rodgers? Peter, I mean. The hounds have to tear the fox to pieces, you see. Well, I mean, they have to *feel* like doing it, don't you know. So we have to be sure to get them in the mood, as it were."

"I never did approve of blood sports," Jonathan said. "Seems to me we might just as well go to bed, Pete old man."

"Fine mess you've managed to get me into," Pete grumbled as they undressed. "If you hadn't gone haring off after Joan Herries . . . come to think of it, if you hadn't come to Kiltone in the first place. Nobody troubled to hit *me* on the head."

"You were quite happy about the idea of getting in here," Jonathan pointed out. "Well, now you're in. Well in." He lay down with a sigh. The bed was soft. He had at last had something to eat, and every muscle and bone in his body seemed to have been through a mangle. He had been up at five this morning, correction, five yesterday morning, to take the car for a test run.

"That was before I knew you were on speaking terms with people like Madame Cantelna." Pete stood at the narrow window, peered out. "Say, she's quite a chick, isn't she?"

"She's also old enough to be our respective mother," Jonathan pointed out. "And as deadly, and as ruthless, as a rattlesnake with ulcers."

"Which is an unkind thing, each of them, to say about a charming and attractive woman," Pete said. "But I agree with your estimate. Would you say we are prisoners? That moat is a long way away."

"Even if either of us was thin enough to squeeze through that window. I'd say we are prisoners, of a sort. But mainly for her amusement."

"Why? Why takes risks like that?"

"What risks? Having us here is a lot safer than letting us roam around Kiltone, once we know *she's* here, wouldn't you say? But let's take a long look at the situation. Starting with the obvious. Anna's being here at all means we're on the right track. The Russians do think, in fact, they must be absolutely sure, that George Herries was Otto Benderer, and that Otto took some paper of value with him out of Germany all those years ago. Maybe Anna does know an old chum of Lord Wantage, but I don't see her coming all the way to Eire just to see a fox hunt. She's running this show."

"I'd go along with that."

"Second point is, she hasn't got what she's looking for, yet. Her pals were at the pub this evening, yesterday evening I mean, offering Ma Herries large sums for the right to search the house. At least, they didn't put it quite so bluntly; they wanted the right to go through all of Otto's papers. Now, as they didn't know I was there yet, there was really no reason for such an involved red herring. The offer must have been genuine."

"What makes your arrival so important?"

"I'll come to that in a moment. My third point is, Anna not only knows that there's something to find, she knows what it is. I'm sure of that. It's just a business of getting at it."

"Because of the offer?"

"For one thing. But there's another. She only permits herself to be amused when she's confident, and right now you have to admit she's in the very best of humors. She figures once she can persuade Ma Herries to unlock the door of old Otto's study, or whatever, she's home and dry. The fourth point is, my gruesome employer, that chap Craufurd we were talking about upstairs, knew all along that Anna was here, which is why he picked me for this job, just to let her know, in his own roundabout fashion, that we were on to her. Of course, it never crossed his mind to tell me anything about it."

"Oh, great," Pete said. "So now I'm bait for some B.S.S. trap."

"Could be. But there's a fifth point, which is linked to number three, her knowing where to look and what to look for. I don't think our showing up has upset Anna in the least. Oh sure, she wants us where she can keep an eye on us, but I don't think she's made up her mind as yet to do anything more than that. I'm not saying Craufurd's little plan isn't going to work. She may feel compelled to get a move on. But she isn't worried that we are going to be able to stop her."

"You mean she isn't going to *let* us stop her," Pete reminded him. "Which to my mind isn't very reassuring for our futures. But if you don't mind, I'll make a couple of points, now." He got into the second bed. "Where there's a bait, there's usually a trap. So if Madame Cantelna is supposed to take fright at your appearance, and start doing things, where's the trap? You notice any of your boys lurking behind bushes?"

"Not one. To tell you the truth, I've never really understood how Craufurd's brain works. I can only tell you that, however convoluted his actions, he usually gets what he wants."

"Yeah? My second point is, what about this Wantage character, and his *Vogue*-type daughter? Darling Dorinda was certainly in on the keeping-us-here act."

"She was indeed. I'm afraid Britain has always thrown up these odd, crazy aristocrats who believe in getting pally with the absolute opposite. There were a lot of them around at the time of the French Revolution, for instance."

"I'll believe that, when it's proved. For my

money, I think old Wantage may be worth investigating, supposing we ever get the chance." Pete switched off the light. "Happy nightmares."

But surprisingly, Jonathan slept without a dream. Although maybe it wasn't so very surprising after all; it seemed only ten seconds before he was awakened by the sound of their bedroom door being opened, and gazed at Clay, who was carefully laying a variety of clothes over the chair.

"Oh, good morning, Mr. Anders," he said. "Although I'm afraid it isn't a very good morning. Spot of drizzle about, and I fancy it may become heavier later on. Good morning to you, Mr. Rodgers. I hope you slept well. Now, I have here some clothes for you to wear to the meet; his lordship thought you might like to try them on. There are some boots here as well. When you are dressed, his lordship would be pleased if you would join him for breakfast, in the great hall in half an hour. Half an hour, if you please, gentlemen. His lordship is very punctual, and the hounds will be ready for the off at eleven."

Pete sat up. "You mean his lordship really expects us to go on this thing?"

"But of course, Mr. Rodgers," Clay said, and closed the door behind him.

"Well, now at least we know what Anna means to do with us," Pete said. "She figures we'll both break our necks, and that will be that."

Jonathan looked at his watch; the time was half past eight. And it *was* a good morning, from his point of view; his head had settled into a dull ache. He got out of bed, washed and shaved, inspected the clothes. They made quite a collection; several pairs of jodhpurs, a choice of three red jackets, five pairs of boots, three hard hats. "I suppose," he said thoughtfully, "there's nothing to stop us mounting up and hightailing it out of here."

"Which would suit her nicely, I imagine," Pete said. "She only wants to keep an eye on us for as long as we're in the vicinity."

"Yeah." Jonathan began trying on jackets. "I've been doing a bit more brooding on it. Remember that we agreed last night that her offer of money to Ma Herries was genuine?"

"Sure do." Pete was inspecting the boots.

"Well, Ma Herries turned her down, and yet Anna is still perfectly happy with the situation. The two things didn't quite jell."

"Do they now?" Pete started to dress as well.

"I think so. Because the offer *wasn't* genuine. It was a try, maybe, and she had to cover a wide field to make her biography story look legitimate, but that idea of opening the coffin to photograph Otto one last time, I mean, how callous can you get. And these are deeply religious, sensitive people. Anna must have known that would put Ma Herries' back up. So obviously she didn't care. She had to keep the pot boiling, give herself a good reason for staying here, so she's negotiating. Because she's just waiting her opportunity to get inside that pub. But she wants to do it secretly."

"Reasonable." Pete brushed his hair. "But in that case, we can stop worrying, because Ma Herries told you there was absolutely nothing in there."

"So she did. But we don't know she was telling the truth. I've an idea that Ma Herries is quite a cute number and is thoroughly enjoying all of us swarming around her like bees at a honeypot. After all, she hinted quite strongly that she was still open to offers."

"So why not make her one."

"What with? I work for the British Government, remember? Anyway, that's not the point I'm trying to make. It occurs to me that if Anna is really just stalling, waiting for an opportunity to get at the pub, what better time can she possibly have than tonight? Tonight's the night everyone in the village comes up to the castle. The first night of the hunt. My bet is that sometime during this evening Anna and her friends will sidle off and do a spot of burglaring."

"And you figure we should stay as close as we can," Pete said.

"I figure we should try," Jonathan said. "Mind you, we don't want to get too close. It's four to two, and those are long odds. And I wouldn't mind betting that they have odd bits of hardware around, too."

"Haven't you?"

"We're not allowed to carry firearms," Jonathan said. "At least, I have never been issued one. What about you?"

"I didn't bring anything. I wanted to play it straight, like a reporter, in case my things were searched. Well then, I guess our first job is to survive today. How do I look?"

"Red suits you. Are we supposed to wear ties with these jackets?"

"I'm going for a turtle neck. I think you have to sort of cover your throat to be correct." Pete put on a hard hat, frowned at himself in the mirror. "You know what I'm going to do? Fall off the moment my horse gets across the bridge. That way I can wave you all good-by and go back to bed."

The great hall seemed crowded. Dorinda Wantage was there, in jodhpurs and boots and a white silk shirt and a blue jacket, looking quite remarkably attractive. But she couldn't match Anna, similarly dressed, and from her utter composure suggesting that she wore riding gear every morning of her life. With them were the three men Jonathan had seen in the Saloon Bar at the Kiltone Arms the previous evening.

"My associates," Anna said. "Tigran, and Ewfim, and Vassily. I won't bother to tell you their last names, as it would merely confuse you. And besides, I'm sure we are all going to be friends. Mr. Jonathan Anders, and Mr. Peter Rodgers. They are agents of their respective governments, come to Kiltone to discover what we are up to."

The three Russians nodded. They looked uncomfortable in their red jackets, as well they might. And dressed, as they were, in identical clothes, it was going to be difficult to tell them apart. Tigran was the largest, and had a huge hooked nose. Ewfim was totally undistinguished, but he smiled a lot. Too much. Vassily was the shortest, but it was only a matter of millimeters; his most distinguishing features were his hands, which were far too small, and white, and delicate.

"Our pleasure," Jonathan said.

"I wish you'd get it straight, Madame Cantelna," Pete protested. "Jon is the agent. I'm the man from *Life,* remember?"

Anna Cantelna's smile was cold. "I think you are the one who should get it straight, Mr. Rodgers.

Surely Jonathan must have told you that I am not exactly a fool? This morning, for instance, Tigran has already been over the road from here to Sligo, and there is no trace of a wrecked car."

"I told you, it disintegrated," Jonathan said.

Anna ignored him. "I have also been on the telephone to the London office of *Life*."

"Now, how did you do that?" Pete asked. "If there's no phone at the castle."

"Dorinda very kindly drove me into the village. And, as you will know, no one at *Life* has ever heard of a Mr. Rodgers, at least on their staff. It would make life so much more simple were we all to be honest with each other, if you will pardon a bad pun."

Pete looked at Jonathan. Jonathan shrugged.

"And this," Dorinda Wantage said, "is Papa. He's been dying to meet you."

Lord Wantage walked from his bedroom across the drawing room and took his seat at the head of the table. Only then did he appear to notice there was anyone else in the room. He was surprisingly old, suggesting that Anna might have been telling the truth when she said he had known her college professor. Like his daughter, he was tall, but unlike her he was very thin; his features were almost emaciated, and from the middle of them a long, sharp nose protruded. He was quite bald, and all in all made Jonathan think of a bird, the resemblance being increased by his tremendously white eyes, for he had the smallest pupils Jonathan had ever seen; they gleamed from a face at least as red as his jacket.

"Come here," he said. "Come here. Glad to meet you, what? Glad to meet you. Sit down. Sit down. You on this side, Mr. Anders. You on this side. And you here, Mr. Rodgers. You here. Secret agents, eh? Secret agents. I like that. Yes. I like that."

Jonathan sat down, and Clay immediately placed an enormous plate of bacon, eggs, mushrooms, fried potatoes, and fried bread in front of him. It reminded him that he was still hungry; he wouldn't be after he got through this little lot, but he'd feel even less like riding a horse.

"I assure you, sir," he said, "we didn't mean to cause you any trouble."

"And you didn't, boy. You didn't. Never even woke me up. Never. Nosing after Anna, are you? Nosing after Anna? All after what that Herries chap left behind, eh? What he left behind. I always thought he was no good. Always thought so. Damned Nazi, what? Damned Nazi. Used to be fond of the Nazis once, myself. Used to be. Met that fellow Hitler, you know. Met that fellow Hitler. Quite impressed. Oh, yes, impressive chap. But had to give it up. Had to give it up. My wife persuaded me. Persuaded me, my wife. Said they were no good. Said they were no good, didn't she, Anna? Didn't she, Anna?"

"Well, they weren't, David. Were they?"

"Oh, you're right there, Anna. You're right. So was my wife. She was right, you know, Mr. Rodgers. She was right. Only woman I've ever met who was always right. Always right. Dorinda is always wrong. Always wrong, you know, Dorinda."

"That's not a very nice thing to say, Papa," Dorinda protested.

"It's the truth, my dear. The truth. Anna tells

me you two boys want to come along on the Meet this morning. The Meet, this morning, eh? Good day for it. Good day. Rain, you see. Rain. The ground will be nice and soft for when you tumble off, what? When you tumble off. I see Clay has found you some clothes. Found you some clothes, eh?"

"Well, actually, Lord Wantage," Pete said, "we'd just as soon watch from the battlements. I bet we'd have a super view from up there. And I have a telephoto lens on my camera."

"You ride to hounds, young man. Ride to hounds. Nothing like it. Nothing like it. Fox hunting is the last truly exciting business in life. The last exciting business, what?"

"Well, I can't agree with that," Jonathan objected. Quite apart from his personal feelings in the matter, his instincts were telling him it was time to start probing; at the moment, Anna Cantelna was just too completely in charge of the situation. "I think it's a beastly business."

"Beastly business?" inquired Lord Wantage, shading from crimson to magenta. "Beastly business? Good heavens. Good heavens! D'you hear that, Dorinda? D'you hear that? D'you hear that, Anna? D'you hear that?"

"I'm afraid I didn't warn you, David," Anna said. "Poor Jonathan is a true representative of the decadent West."

"For crying out loud," Pete protested. "Then what would you call his lordship here?"

"What would you call yourself, David?"

"What? What? Decadent? Me? Decadent? What

rubbish. Absolute rubbish. I ride to hounds, boy. Ride to hounds. There's your decadence. There's your decadence."

"I couldn't agree more," Jonathan said.

"And you also entertain Commies in your house," Pete pointed out. "No offense, Madame Cantelna, but you'll admit that oil and water don't generally mix."

"Communists?" shouted Lord Wantage. "Communists? Anna is an old friend, sir. An old friend."

"She'd have you out of this castle of yours in five minutes if she was running things."

"What? What?"

"Mr. Rodgers is theorizing," Anna said with a smile. "I am not running things, perhaps fortunately for you, Mr. Rodgers. And I at least have the manners not to quarrel with my host."

"You're upsetting Papa," Dorinda said severely.

"The hunt," declared Lord Wantage. "The hunt. By Gad, sir, the hunt. By Gad. We'll make men out of you yet, sir. Make men, we will."

He left the table and headed for the stairs, somewhat uncertainly. The three Russians also rose, and waited for instructions from their leader.

Anna smiled at Jonathan. "Shall we go?"

Jonathan followed Tigran, who was walking behind Anna.

The big man leaned forward. "Today," he muttered in Russian. "Today is a good day, eh, Anna?"

"I think so, Tigran. I think so." She turned to smile at Jonathan. "We are looking forward to the hunt," she said in English. "I am quite excited."

He tried to remember; but there was no reason

for her to know that amongst the many subjects Harold Indman had made him study was spoken Russian. He descended the stairs at her elbow. "I wonder if it would be possible for you and me to have a little chat, Anna. Somewhere nice and quiet. And just us."

"Why, Jonathan, what a charming idea. Did you know that you have always been my favorite Englishman, no matter what may have happened in the past? What would we talk about?"

Jonathan sighed. "I thought we might compare notes. We're both after the same thing, aren't we?"

"The fox, you mean, Jonathan? Why, of course we are. But I would say, as we are both new to the game, we should follow the examples set by those who are more experienced. As to finding him, I am told there is no problem there. The hounds always flush him out of hiding."

"Okay," he said. "If that's the way you want to play it. I just thought, as you haven't got very far I would say, that you might like to pool information."

She paused on the last landing before the garage. Below them they could hear the dogs barking and whining. "And you have something to offer in that direction, Jonathan?"

"I might have. I might be able to guarantee you a way home afterward."

"Meaning that you stopped me the last time, beat me, and humiliated me? Oh, I haven't forgotten that, Jonathan. I often lie awake at night and remember my last visit to these islands. But neither you nor Mr. Craufurd can touch me in Eire."

"I wouldn't be too sure of that."

She gave him a quick glance. But she could not

be certain he was bluffing. She had thought he was bluffing all the while on their last meeting. And most of the time he *had* been bluffing. But things had fallen into his lap.

"Perhaps you could convince me, Jonathan. Just a little."

He had already decided that his best course was to keep stirring, in the hopes of destroying her confidence. He remembered that once Anna became nervous, she also became only half as determined, half as dangerous. "Well," he said. "Suppose I told you that I know your plans for this evening? When the do starts up here at the castle, you're meaning to push off with your three friends and do a loot on the pub. I may as well tell you that I mean to stop you."

She gazed at him for several seconds. "Do you now, Jonathan," she said softly. "I shall have to think about what you say. But after the hunt."

The dogs, Jonathan was glad to see, had been reconfined in their cage; they barked and leaped against the wire netting, obviously anxious to get on with it. Lord Wantage was already mounted, and six other horses stood waiting, held by two grooms.

"Hey, Jonathan," Pete whispered. "Do you see what I see?"

The grooms were George and Joe.

"Well, like the man said, it's a small village."

Dorinda mounted next, and then Anna, and then the three Russians.

"You'll see I've reserved the two most docile mounts we have for you and Mr. Anders, Peter," Dorinda said. "I wonder why I bothered."

"Yeah," Pete said, and approached his horse. "The top of the morning to you, George."

"And to ye, Mr. Rodgers," George said. "Had a good night's sleep, did ye?"

"Middling. What do I do?"

"Bend your knee, Mr. Rodgers, and I'll give ye a boost."

A moment later Pete was seated, more or less firmly.

"Now tell us the truth, Mr. Anders," Joe whispered. "How ever did ye manage to get out of them caves? Paddy swears ye must still be wandering around in there."

"But you'll put him right about that," Jonathan said.

"Ah, he'll see for himself, Mr. Anders. The whole village comes to the hunt."

"You mean Mick'll be there as well?"

"Sure, and they couldn't have the hunt without Mick. He'll be very glad to see ye again. Oh, yes. He was afraid ye might have run off into Ulster, and ye see, the council in Sligo upheld the sentences. Mick's wanting to have the executions."

"I love you, too," Jonathan said, and settled in the saddle.

"If you are quite ready, Mr. Anders," Lord Wantage remarked. "Quite ready. Then we shall be off. Be off, what? What?"

Clay was standing by to open the gate, and his lordship led the procession across the bridge and onto the drive, where there was a considerable crowd already accumulated, despite the steady downpour of rain. The first person Jonathan saw was Mick, wearing a coat and a top hat and carrying a trumpet. There were also several other mounted men and women, clearly gentry from the neighboring villages. Parked on either side of the drive were a double row of gigs and carts, each with its horse patiently waiting. At the very end, there were several cars, including Tim's taxi, and Tim himself, together with all the older folk Jonathan had seen in the pub the previous night, and the courting couple he had disturbed in the saloon bar. Kathleen Herries was there too, wearing her raincoat and with her head bound up in a black scarf. But there was no sign of Joan and Pat. He wondered if Pete was disappointed. But Pete had moved to the front and was talking to Dorinda Wantage. He certainly did not believe in letting the moments waste away.

Lord Wantage had halted his mount in the very center of the assembly and was talking at large, repeating everything, as usual. Meanwhile Clay, followed by the two grooms, was leaving the castle gate with stately tread; each carried a tray laden with glasses of red wine. These were offered not only to the waiting huntsmen and the ladies, but also to the onlookers. It occurred to Jonathan that Lord Wantage certainly knew how to make himself popular with the locals, however much he might despise them. Jonathan drank his wine, and felt a little more secure in the saddle. He kicked his horse and got it to walk across to Mrs. Herries.

"Why, Mr. Anders," she cried. "D'ye know, I thought it must be ye, but in a red coat and all. And that hat on your head. And why did ye up and leave me house last night? Joan said ye'd had a telegram. Something about a bereavement."

"Something did come up," he agreed. "And we thought, at one time, that it *was* going to involve a bereavement. Or even two. But fortunately, things weren't so bad as they had appeared. And then we met Lord Wantage, and he insisted we come along on this hunt."

"Ah, ye'll enjoy the hunt, Mr. Anders. Ye'll enjoy the hunt." She was starting to sound like the old man. "And ye must keep an eye out for Joan. She's somewhere along the way, looking out for ye."

"I'll do that. Tell me, Mrs. Herries, you'll be coming up to the castle for the reception tonight?"

"But of course she will, Jonathan," Anna Cantelna said. There was so much noise and bustle and clipclopping of hooves that he hadn't heard her behind him. "Everyone comes up to the castle on the first night of the hunt. Lord Wantage is a very democratic man, despite your rude remarks."

"Oh, he's democratic, all right," Kathleen Herries agreed. "I'll be there. Ye'll be the Russian lady?"

"Yes," Anna said. "I am truly sorry we have not managed to meet before, Mrs. Herries. I feel sure that had I come down personally to see you we'd have been able to come to some arrangement. Sadly, I haven't been very well since arriving in Kiltone. But I'm much better now. We must have a long chat tonight."

Kathleen Herries smiled. "Aye. Aye. Ye'll be bidding against each other, will ye? I'll look forward to that."

Anna turned her horse. "You weren't trying to persuade her to keep away tonight, were you, Jonathan? You would never have succeeded. Everyone in Kiltone will be up at the castle on the first night of the hunt. There will be drinking and music and merrymaking from tea time until dawn, just about. Why, there is even an orchestra coming in from Sligo. The village will be as deserted as a ghost town. Isn't that a lovely thought? I think David is ready to start."

She urged her horse away from his side, left him frowning after her. Confidence was one thing Anna Cantelna had never lacked. But this time she seemed to be deliberately teasing him, throwing down a challenge. Because, of course, she had strength on her side. Clay would have searched their bags while he unpacked them last night, and would have been able to tell her they were not armed. And so it was just the two of them against her three extremely large assistants.

But she'd had even greater strength on her side the last time; he'd have thought she would be remembering that.

With a howling and a wailing, the hounds, just released by George, came flooding over the bridge, rushing to and fro. Lord Wantage raised his hat, and Mick rose in his stirrups and blew a loud blast on his horn. The hounds were already careering down the drive and through the now-opened gates, and the cavalcade moved behind, some already breaking into a gallop. The more prudent, among them Pete and Jonathan, remained at a gentle canter. Behind the riders, in turn, the onlookers piled into the horse-drawn carts and moved down the drive and onto the road. They were making for the top of the hill, where the whole of the downs would be displayed beneath them. The hounds went straight across the road and onto the field beyond; their first destination was the small copse Jonathan had seen from the battlements the previous night. The hunt followed. Next to the road was the first problem, a low stile. Jonathan watched Lord Wantage take it like a steeplechaser, leaning back in his saddle, with Anna immediately behind him. Of course, horse riding was still a fairly common pastime in Russia.

Mick had cast back to whip up the stragglers. "Heels down, Mr. Anders," he bellowed. "Keep your heels down. We don't want ye to break your neck, now, do we?"

"It'd save ammunition," Jonathan gasped, dug his heels downward and found that it did seem to anchor him more firmly in the saddle. The hedge rushed at him, and he decided to leave all decisions to the horse, which had surely done this sort of thing before. For a long moment there seemed to be no earth left at all, and it was next stop the moon. Then he landed with a jar which sent his backbone clear through his hard hat, and felt himself rising again, where the horse was not.

"Heels down!" Mick bawled, still just behind him.

Jonathan obeyed and sank back into the saddle, while his mount charged across the open ground toward the wood. He looked around and saw Pete about fifty yards to his left, riding close to an elderly lady in a blue jacket, both hands on the reins, only releasing them every few seconds in order to push his glasses back up his nose.

The hounds were by now already into the

bracken and out again, with a curiously high-pitched wailing to denote that they had flushed the fox from his lair. Jonathan could not see the animal, but already the leading riders were debouching from the trees and streaming across the next field. The tail-enders promptly seized their opportunity to by-pass the drooping branches altogether and swing away to the left hand of the copse, hoping to regain the main body. Mick led this rear section. So Jonathan, finding himself last, pulled his reins to the right, leaving the others, and charged away.

In a matter of seconds he was out of sight of the rest, although he could still hear the baying of the hounds and the blare of Mick's trumpet. His problem was which way to go now. He raised his head and gave a hasty glance around, and saw Joan Herries and her friend Pat peering at him from the top of a rise perhaps fifty yards farther to his right.

Desperately he sawed the reins once again, leaning back and throwing all his weight into his shoulders. The horse stopped so promptly that Jonathan went sliding backward out of the saddle and lost a stirrup. Then just as suddenly the disgusted animal started off again, lowering its head as it did so. Jonathan was catapulted forward like a bullet from a gun, shot over the horse's head, landed on his feet, and took a couple of running strides before he collapsed on his face and rolled over several times.

He found himself on his back, gazing at the clouds which seemed immediately above his head, and was for the first time grateful for the drizzle, which was refreshing on his face and had made the ground reasonably soft.

The two girls came running across the meadow toward him.

"There!" Pat cried. "I told ye it was Mr. Anders."

"And ye were right, as usual," Joan panted. "But whatever are ye doing on the back of a horse, Mr. Anders?"

"Was he doing, ye mean," Pat pointed out and giggled.

"And in his lordship's hunt and all," Joan said.

"It's a long story." Jonathan wiped mud from his face.

"And Mr. Rodgers?" Joan asked. "Is he riding with them, too?"

"If he's still up, he's still riding. Somewhere over there." Jonathan waved his hand. "Now tell me, what made you two girls decide to watch the hunt from this particular place?"

"Oh, we always watch from around here," Pat said. "The fox always makes for the copse when he hears the hounds, ye see. So we get a good view of the start, anyway."

"And of your finish." Joan seemed amused. "Man, Mr. Anders, ye came off in brilliant style."

"Pity you didn't have a camera." He got up. The ground kept on moving for a few minutes, but apparently he had suffered nothing worse than a few bruises, although his head was banging away all over again. "As it happens, I fell off because I was trying to stop the beast. I wanted to talk with you."

"With us, Mr. Anders?" Joan asked.

"Yes. I need your help."

"Again?" Pat asked.

"Listen, we may be on different sides of that border over there, but you'll agree that we all have to oppose the Communists."

"Well, now, I've never thought about that," Joan said. "Anyway, there aren't any Communists around Kiltone."

"Don't you believe it. There are four of them staying at the castle."

"Ye mean those Russians?"

"Sure and me father does say all Russians are Communists," Pat said. "It's to do with their religion, see?"

"Russians don't have a religion," Joan explained. "It's because they're Communists."

"Listen," Jonathan begged. "They're here to get your father's papers. The ones that are locked up in his desk."

Joan frowned at him. "Sure and ye took a nasty fall, Mr. Anders. Ye'd better let me call for Tim and his taxi."

"Listen," Jonathan said again. "There's no need to keep that up any more. Do it if you must, but just listen. Tonight, when everybody in the village is going to be up at the castle enjoying themselves, Madam Cantelna and her three friends are going to take your mother's inn apart. And I bet they'll leave a mess. And they're going to find your dad's papers, no matter where they're hidden. Now there's very little Pete and I can do about it, by ourselves, but we thought it might be nice if you were to get hold of your trigger-happy boyfriends and stop them."

"And where do ye come into it, Mr. Anders? Daddy was a German."

"All of that was before I was born, sweetheart. I'd like to have those papers myself. That's up to you. But far more important than that is to stop the Russians from getting them."

"Aye," Pat said. "Aye."

"There's something else," Jonathan said. "I'd be grateful if you could go to the post office and telephone the newspaper office in Sligo, and see what you can find out about Lord Wantage."

"Sure and that'll be no trouble for Joan," Pat assured him. "Mrs. Herries is the postmistress and all. But why d'ye want to inquire about his lordship? And ye staying with him and all? *He* can't be a Communist."

"He's a very odd fellow, wouldn't you say?"

"Ah, well, he is that. A lord, ye see, Mr. Anders."

"That doesn't excuse everything," Jonathan reminded her. "Will you help me, Joan?"

Joan was still considering the matter. "Mr. Rodgers is with ye?"

"Completely."

"Aye," Pat said. "Aye. Oh, my lord!"

"Got ye," said a familiarly angry voice. "Just stand up wi' your hands up, Mr. Anders."

Paddy stood above them, complete with shotgun.

CHAPTER 5

He made a formidable figure, standing above them on a slight hummock, wearing a cape and an ex-service peaked cap, looming through the rain. Presumably it was the constant downpour which had enabled him to approach them unheard.

"Ah, Paddy O'Rourke," Pat complained. "Ye're always appearing at the wrong time and causing trouble."

"Maybe ye don't understand," Paddy informed her. "Maybe ye're of the opinion that we let these two fellows go last night. Sure and they got away by themselves. How, I cannot say. But away they went, and me left sitting there all by me lonesome, and looking mighty stupid. So for a start, I'll have Mr. Anders back where he belongs, in that cave."

"Listen," Jonathan said. "I was just trying to explain to these two young ladies that I really was not interested in your smuggling. I'm after something quite different. Far more important."

"Well, ye can try your luck with Mick, when he

gets back from the fox. Come on, now, or I'll blast ye, here and now. Ye can shoot the pair of them on sight, Mick told me, if they give ye any trouble. They're condemned men. And if it was not for the girls being here I'd be after doing just that. So be off wi' the pair of ye."

"Oh, Paddy, I'm sure ye don't mean it," Joan said.

"Be off wi' ye," Paddy growled.

"I think you'd better do as the man says," Jonathan decided. "He looks pretty angry. And don't worry, I shouldn't think he'll shoot me right this minute. For one thing, Mick told him to get the pair of us, and Pete is still galloping around Ireland. And for another thing, the hunt might hear."

"The hunt?" Paddy asked contemptuously. "Sure and they're in the next county by now. Ye did us a right good turn by falling off."

"Well," Joan said, "ye do Mr. Anders an injury, and I'll not speak to ye again before Christmas. Come on, Pat. Like he says, the hounds won't be back for a while. Ma'll have hot coffee in her cart."

"And think about what I was saying," Jonathan suggested.

Joan glanced at him, and then set off across the fields, followed by Pat.

"Christmas," Paddy said to himself, obviously working it out. "Sure and that's only a few weeks off. Now let's get on with it."

Jonathan sighed. Actually, he thought things might be looking up; there was a better than even chance that Joan and Pat believed him and would help him. It was only a matter of their getting round

109

their menfolk. And of all the menfolk, the most difficult would certainly be Paddy. But he was a large chap, and he had the gun.

"Okay," he said. "Okay. Do you want me to clasp my hands on the back of my head?"

"Now, why would ye be after doing that?" Paddy wanted to know.

"I just want to be sure I'm doing the right thing," Jonathan said. The girls had by now disappeared, and they were alone in the teeming rain. "Hey, I thought you said the hunt was in the next county?"

"At the least," Paddy said.

"So what's the fox doing back over here then?"

"Eh? Eh?" Paddy's head turned in the direction of Jonathan's gaze, and Jonathan clasped both hands together and swung the combined fist sideways, landing the blow just above Paddy's left ear. Over he went, splashing into the mud. It was the sort of blow which would have laid most men out, but Paddy appeared to be more surprised than hurt. Jonathan had to dive after him to get his hands on the shotgun. For a moment they wrestled with it, both on their knees. "Sure, Mr. Anders," Paddy admitted, "and I did not expect a gentleman like ye to know about scrapping. I'm going to have to clobber ye." He took his right hand away from the barrel and closed it into a fist. Jonathan made a supreme effort, tore the gun free, and was struck by a tremendous swinging right-handed blow, which in turn sent him sprawling in the mud. He lost his grip on the shotgun, which went skidding beyond his reach.

"So ye want to fight," Paddy said, weaving to

and fro with his fists raised. "So come on, ye English nutter. Up ye get. And put your hands up."

Jonathan scrambled to his feet, and Paddy came at him, left hand whipping in and out, right bobbing about under his chin. But Jonathan concluded that no doubt he had had a very good reason for giving up the ring before it had given him up instead. His movements were mechanical, and the first left hand that got through was more of a push than a punch. Still, it was hard enough to cause Jonathan to lose his balance once again, and down he slipped on the muddy turf.

"Come on, come on," Paddy bawled, circling around him. "If it's a fight ye're after, I'm your man. Come on, come on."

Jonathan sat up, propelled himself forward, and threw both arms around Paddy's waist.

"Hey," bawled the boxer, falling over with a splash. "Ye can't do that."

Jonathan got himself free, rose to his knees, and used his two-handed blow again, back and forth, each shifting Paddy's head—but so far as he could see, causing more harm to his own hands than to the Irishman.

"Why, Mr. Anders," Dorinda Wantage asked. "Whatever are you doing?"

She had walked her horse from the copse, and now stood above them while the rain dripped from the brim of her hard hat.

Jonathan got to his feet. "Paddy and I were having a little argument."

"Paddy O'Rourke?" Dorinda asked. "Is that you

beneath all that mud? Well, really! What a way to behave on the first day of the season. Now be off with you. If your mother sees you this dirty she'll take a stick to your back, I shouldn't wonder. And I wouldn't blame her at all."

Paddy also got up, looking remarkably shamefaced. "Can I get me gun back first, Miss Dorinda?"

"If you leave it there, it'll surely rust," she pointed out. "I don't suppose you have any idea where your horse is, Mr. Anders?"

"I'm afraid he kept on going when I came off."

"He'll have gone home, I suppose. He hates the rain. You'll have to mount up behind me."

"I can walk," Jonathan said.

"Oh, nonsense. Then you'll be catching cold on top of everything else. Come on, now, upsadaisy." She gave him her hand, and a brisk pull had him astride behind her. "You have to put your arms round my waist," she instructed. "Well, I'll say good morning to you, Paddy. We'll see you at the castle tonight, I hope?"

Paddy touched his forehead. "I'll be there, Miss Dorinda."

He remained, leaning on his shotgun, watching them disappear over the next rise.

"He's rather a sweet boy," Dorinda remarked. "But quick-tempered. It really was a mistake for you to start fighting him; he once boxed an eliminator for the middleweight title."

"And lost, I imagine," Jonathan said. "But many thanks for happening along. I have a vague idea that you may have saved me from quite a shellacking. What brought you back this way?"

"I suddenly noticed that you were no longer with us," she said. "I thought you might have hurt yourself. It certainly never crossed my mind that you'd be fighting with the locals."

"It's an involved story."

"Well, then," she said. "Are you sitting comfortably?"

"As comfortably as can be expected. This is a remarkably bony horse. But I'm afraid a fair amount of my mud is coming off on your coat."

"That was inevitable," she pointed out.

"And on your hair." It kept blowing in his face, although the horse was only walking.

"I always wash it after a meet, anyway. Tell me about Paddy."

What did he have to lose? However closely linked she was to Anna Cantelna, she certainly seemed able to control the wild Irish; and failing Joan, Mick and the boys were going to remain a problem.

"Oh, well, Pete Rodgers and I went investigating last night and stumbled upon your young Irish friends smuggling guns up the coast there. They took exception to this, got hold of us, and actually condemned us to death."

"Good heavens," she said. "Is that where you got your bump on the head?"

"As a matter of fact, yes. But as you know, we managed to get away from them, which is actually why we showed up at the castle looking for shelter. But it seems half the blessed I.R.A. in this vicinity work for your old man."

"From time to time," she agreed. "There's no industry around here, except fishing. But we believe in keeping in with the locals, as you'll have observed. If you're good, we may manage to have your sentence commuted from death to life imprisonment. We can always keep the pair of you in our dungeon. It's quite warm down there, really; that's where the boiler is. And I could come down and talk to you, every day. Would you like that?"

"You're a real comedian."

"Of course," she reminded him. "That would depend on your telling me the truth. I mean, I'd want to know the real reason why you came to Kiltone. And Mr. Rodgers? Was it the I.R.A., or poor Anna?"

Jonathan watched the towers of Kiltone Castle rising over the next hummock. The hilltop to their left was empty now; having seen the hunt away, the villagers had retired from the rain, no doubt to the shelter of Mrs. Herries' pub to start celebrating early.

And Dorinda Wantage had returned to look for him. To make sure he hadn't taken the opportunity to clear off? Hardly likely, or even important, when Pete was still very much around. It occurred to him that perhaps Anna was not so well placed, or that he was not as badly placed as they both imagined.

"Well, Mr. Anders?"

"I might," he said. "In exchange for some information from you."

"What on earth could I have to tell you?"

"Well, your old man is rather odd, don't you think?"

"You don't really expect me to agree with you? Because that would mean that I am also rather odd."

She urged her horse through the still-open gates onto the drive.

"In the pleasantest possible fashion, I'm sure. That is, supposing you share his point of view. If I knew what it was, I might be able to agree with it too."

"I shouldn't think so," she said. "Papa is an individualist. He is unhappy about the way the world is going."

"Aren't we all?"

"But you are helping it on its way, Mr. Anders. Although, come to think of it, in view of everything that has happened, I'd like to start calling you Jonathan. Do you mind if I call you Jonathan?"

"I'd like you to."

"And you must call me Dorinda. As I was saying, you are an active, I imagine an eager, participant in the downward slide. Papa has opted out. I mean, what a stupid way to live, having to be either a Conservative or a Socialist, a Democrat or a Republican, a Communist or an anti-Communist, even a Protestant or a Catholic."

"I couldn't agree with you more," Jonathan said. "Providing everybody, or at least a substantial majority, felt that way. As almost everybody feels quite the opposite, you *have* to choose."

"The more usual phrase is stand up and be counted," Dorinda pointed out. "Daddy has done just that. Out."

"No one can just turn their back on the problems of the world."

"Anyone can, if they have enough money."

"And what about the responsibilities of having

115

money, and position? I presume he is a member of the House of Lords, whether he likes it or not. What about his responsibilities, as a member of one of the wealthy nations to assist the developing countries? What about all the people who are starving, who would starve in even greater numbers were we all to adopt your Dad's point of view? What about the plain fact of his being British, and sitting in a village which smuggles arms for the express purpose of causing trouble in a part of Britain. I imagine he's quite happy to use a British passport."

"Shall I take your points in order?" she asked, apparently unperturbed. "In the first place, the powers of the House of Lords have been so reduced over the past fifty years it's not worth belonging to it. In the second place, if England does happen still to be a wealthy nation, which is a point of view not everyone accepts, it wasn't always, and it became one entirely by its own efforts. I think I would be right in saying that India, just for example, was a great empire while we were still savages, and I don't remember ever reading about their sharing any of their wealth with us, voluntarily. In the third place, large numbers of the world's population have always starved, from time to time. It's a natural law. Time was when a bad harvest meant a lot of English people were starving, and starvation isn't something you want to mention in Ireland. Oh, no, no. Papa has only one rule for life: Never interfere with nature's laws. As for passports, they happen to be necessary. Nuisances, but then, all man-made laws are nuisances."

"It's very convenient for your old man to make rules about not disturbing nature. Hasn't it ever occurred to you that someone must have interfered with nature once, to make him this wealthy?"

"Our family has been accumulating money for years. For centuries, in fact. That is obeying a dictate of nature. Accumulate strength, because only the strong survive. Money is the muscle of civilization. Now, supposing all my ancestors had been careful to marry only strong, beautiful women—or men, as the case might be—and thus produced in time an unusually beautiful and strong breed of children. Would you say that was interfering with nature? That would be natural selection carried to a logical conclusion." She halted her horse on the drawbridge and turned round to smile at him. "At which point, you're supposed to say, I thought that's what they had done, looking at you."

"Oh, I'm sure they did." Jonathan climbed down. "I'd like to argue with you a while about their point of view, but I suppose it'll have to keep. I would like to point out to you, though, that Anna Cantelna's presence here means that *she's* interfering with nature."

Dorinda Wantage also dismounted. "In what way? She's an old friend of Daddy's; of mine, too, now; I think she's absolutely charming."

"Interfering with nature is her profession," Jonathan said.

"Oh, I don't altogether agree with everything she does, or says. But in my opinion it would be wrong of me to try to stop her. Let people get on with it. That's the Wantage motto."

The castle gate opened. Clay had apparently been watching their approach. "Back so soon, Miss

Dorinda? Ah, there you are, Mr. Anders. Your horse returned about an hour ago, and we concluded that you must have fallen off."

"I got off, if you must know. And now, I'd like a hot bath."

"Clay will run it for you." Dorinda led him up the stairs to the floor containing the guest bedrooms. "And perhaps he should have a look at your head, as well. And your face." She paused on the next flight. "Of course, you know, although I should never interfere with Anna, there's no reason why you shouldn't, if that happens to be your job. It *is* your job, isn't it?" She leaned her head on the wall and smiled at him. "I might even help you, just a little. If I thought you'd appreciate it properly. Living in Kiltone is a very lonely business."

She was a surprising, and a disturbing, young woman; her already attractive looks were strangely increased by her utterly nihilistic point of view. In any event, beggars can't be choosers, Jonathan reasoned. To stop Anna now, he would need all the help he could get. Although when he was overtired, as now, he didn't really see what good the Brigade of Guards would be, camped on the drive.

He had a good soak in a steaming tub, allowed Clay to apply antiseptic ointment to his bruised face, and lay down on his bed. If possible, he was more tired and was suffering more aches and pains than the previous night. Correction, it was only that morning, and tonight promised to be just as exhausting.

And always there was Anna, composed and confident. There was so much to be considered, so much to be worked out. Already he was distrusting his reasoning of last night and this morning, however logical it all seemed when arranged in order. Certainties: that George Herries was Otto Benderer, that he had been working on something to do with the sea—or why send Anna Cantelna at all; but in any event, why send someone as important as Anna? Because it all had to be in code or formula of some sort, and only Anna would be able instantly to recognize it. All logical.

And it was just as logical that if she could not obtain Otto Benderer's papers by fair means, then she would use foul. Except that . . .

He was awakened at four by Pete stamping into the room. "Boy, that was some ride. If my legs ever get straight again, it'll be a miracle."

"Did you catch the fox?"

"I was there to see *them* catch the fox, if that's what you mean. Ugh! Like you said, it's not an edifying sport. But old nutcase Wantage seems happy enough. He's brandishing the brush around, as if he means to use it on any hair he has left. But what's been happening with yourself? Rumor has it you returned doubled up with the gorgeous Dorinda. If you follow me."

"Gorgeous just about sums her up," Jonathan said, and told him about his meeting with the two girls, and Paddy O'Rourke, and about his rescue by Dorinda. But he decided against repeating any of their conversation. From what he had seen Pete was perfectly capable of finding out the truth about Dorinda Wantage for himself.

"Anyway," Pete said, getting beneath the hot

shower, "it's all change for luncheon cum high tea, followed by an endless wassail. It's going to be some night. In the midst of which, you reckon, Anna and her boys will make their play."

"That's how it figures," Jonathan agreed. "Nothing else makes sense. And yet there's something about the way Anna is playing this that is giving me the heebie-jeebies. You know, it's all as clear as you could wish, and yet not quite clear enough; like looking through unfocused binoculars. Try this, just for instance. George Herries died last Saturday, and the news about who he really was hit the press on Monday morning. Let's say it got to Moscow about Monday lunchtime, wheels were put into motion, and Anna was on her way by Tuesday afternoon. She showed up yesterday morning. No, that can't be right. Today's Friday. Or am I dreaming?"

"We lost an entire day, remember?" Pete pointed out. "She actually showed up on Wednesday morning. That's the day before yesterday."

"Having wangled an invitation to stay with old Wantage. So Wednesday afternoon she sent her goons down to chat up Ma Herries."

"I'm beginning to get your drift," Pete said. "You mean, why didn't she go herself?"

"No, I think that's plain enough. She was afraid there might still be reporters around, and one of them might have taken a snap of her. That would have told everybody this was no newspaper team. My point is, on Wednesday they were just reconnoitering, and they got no change out of Ma Herries, in any case. Yesterday they offered her cash for Otto's papers, which is a logical step, and then tossed in that hideous bit about permission to open his grave to take a photograph, which is totally illogical."

"Because they *wanted* her to refuse them, you said. They were just marking time, waiting for tonight, when they can virtually help themselves. Surely *that's* logical enough."

"The point is, when they arranged their visit here, they didn't *know* about the first day of the Meet, or about Wantage's habit of holding open house. They couldn't have."

"They'd have learned about it the moment they got here," Pete said.

"Granted. But that's not Anna's way. She would never have traveled all this distance on spec. She came here with a clear plan, which had nothing to do with the hunt. I'd bet a million on that."

"Maybe she did. But then she changed her mind when old man Wantage offered her an empty village. So what she originally meant to do no longer matters."

"I wish we could be sure of that. Here's something else. Early this morning you and I show up. Now whether that bothered her or not, she wasn't going to let us see it, and with Dorinda's help she managed to keep us here. But she must have brooded on it, just a little. Yet this morning, after breakfast, I overheard Tigran saying to her that today was a good day. For the big loot? So it is, but why mention it if they'd already planned to use tonight? And why not a word like, what are we going to do with those two fellows? Anna doesn't know I understand Russian, so I'm sure it wasn't a wool-pulling job. You follow me? Everything makes sense, on the surface, and yet it doesn't make sense at all when you start to take it apart. It's enough to drive a chap up the wall."

"I think you're just overanxious because it happens to be the Cantelna dame. Sure, respect her, but don't let's start making her more brilliant, or more involved, than she is. So something happened last night to make this an especially good day. I'll tell you what it was. You and I walked into their arms. Anna wasn't bluffing last night; she was as pleased as punch. She had to know there'd be a British agent knocking around, but she didn't know who or where until you drifted in, complete with her American problem. You said your friend Craufurd wanted to stir things up? Well, in my opinion he just sorted things out, for Anna."

"Maybe. But I've just remembered something else that happened last night. Mick and the boys brought in a load of ammunition."

"Ow! And you've just asked Joan to get them to help *us*. But that's absurd, old man. Mick and the boys may not like you very much, but I'd bet *my* last dollar they would never dream of playing along with Anna and her moujiks. Anyway, would she need them, or dare risk using them? And another thing, surely they'd have known the guns were coming in last night for a heck of a long time. Tide tables are printed for a whole year, and this is October. I'd bet those boys have a visitor just about every spring tide, and every one is marked off on Mick's calendar, and has been since last Christmas."

"I suppose you're right," Jonathan muttered. "So in that respect, maybe Anna was unlucky in having to arrive here just as the tides were coming up to full. Now there's another point. Assuming, and I *am* assuming, that she arrived with a foolproof scheme for getting at Otto's papers, her local agent—for you can be sure she has one—would have warned her that Kiltone is a gunrunning center every spring tide. So she had to wait until after the guns had arrived, as she just couldn't afford to have all those young fellows breathing down her neck. But now, why? It's all systems go."

"Still not right, because I'd have said that *last* night was the ideal occasion to do her bit of burglary," Pete objected. "With all the village youth accumulated on the cliffs."

"Ah, but all the old people were accumulated in the pub. Answer that one."

"For pity's sake, we could bat theories to and fro all night. I'd say the only thing we can do is stick closer to Anna than a pair of leeches." Pete finished dressing and moved to the window. "Say, things must be happening. All those cars and traps are back. What a lousy night. You know something else that has changed, but good, since yesterday? The weather. Well, Clay, old man, what can we do for you?"

The butler bowed. "His lordship is awaiting your presence in the great hall, gentlemen."

There was standing room only. Lord Wantage beamed upon the assembly from the head of the dining table, which was entirely covered with bottles of champagne and plates of cold meats and salads. He wore a mauve dinner jacket over a frilled green shirt and a pink bow tie. He was an individualist with no color sense. He said, "Well, Anders? Well, Anders, what? What? Came off at the copse, did you? Off at the copse, eh? Well, what? What, Rodgers? Rodgers? In at the death, eh? At the death. Good man. Good man. Brilliant ride, what? Brilliant ride."

Dorinda wore an off-the-shoulder red satin evening gown. "Peter," she said. "I'm so glad to see you back, safe and sound." But she had apparently made *her* decision. "Why, Jonathan," she said softly, taking her place beside him. "I had hoped that you'd come up early and have a drink with me. We have so much to talk about."

"It took me longer than I'd expected, getting that mud off," he explained. "But I'm here now."

Anna Cantelna wore a green velvet pants suit and black boots. "Jonathan," she admonished. "They tell me you fell off. I hope you didn't hurt yourself?"

"Just a few bruises."

"And one on your face," she smiled. "Almost as if someone hit you. You will keep on falling out with people. But I do hope you are going to ask me to dance, Jonathan. I'd like that."

"I'm going to dance with you all evening, Anna," Jonathan promised, and spotted her three friends, looking vaguely uncomfortable in dinner jackets and clustered in a corner, as usual.

"Mr. Anders!" Kathleen Herries wore a black evening gown. "Ah, George must be sorry to be missing this. He looked forward to the first night of the Hunt, he always did. Made me promise to come to this one, the night before he died. Mind ye, Mr. Anders, he never rode to hounds. He was no horseman. And ye fell off. Ah, ye have to watch the copse.

Many's the good rider come to grief near there. Ah, yes. A treacherous spot."

Jonathan sighed. "I'm quite all right, Mrs. Herries, really."

Mick wore corduroy, in pale red. "Man, Mr. Anders. Sure and I was that worried when I didn't see ye up at the kill. Ye know, I was afraid for a moment that ye'd run off to Sligo or some such place. Which would be most unfortunate, because we've fixed the execution and all."

"George told me you'd worked something out," Jonathan said.

"And Paddy here tried to get ye back on his own. But ye dusted him up, he says."

"Sure and I misjudged the fellow entirely." Paddy wore a dinner jacket, and might have been about to referee the Big Fight. "He can swap punches with the best. Made my head swing, he did. But he don't fight fair."

"Catch-as-catch-can stuff, eh?" Mick asked. "That's the best way, Mr. Anders. The best way. Sure and I'll tell no lie; I'll be sorry to see ye go."

"Listen," Jonathan said. "Joking apart. Didn't Joan have a word with you?"

"Sure, I was on at him." Joan wore the shortest skirt Jonathan had seen in a long time. But she had the legs for it. And Pete was in close attendance, as usual. "He won't take me seriously."

"Let me have a go at him," Pete volunteered.

"Sure, Mr. Rodgers, and I don't doubt that ye have your problems," Mick said. "But why should me boys help ye? I don't see ye doing much to help us."

"Sssh," Pat hissed. In contrast to her friend, she wore a black midi-skirt which made her look like a witch. "His lordship is going to speak."

Lord Wantage had clapped for silence and was now waving the fox's brush to and fro. "Ladies," he said. "Ladies and gentlemen. Gentlemen, what? Allow me to welcome you to Kiltone Castle. Welcome to Kiltone Castle, what? At the start of another hunting season. Another hunting season, what? And a successful start, what? Successful." He waved the brush some more. "I am particularly happy, particularly happy, to welcome so many distinguished guests from overseas. Guests from overseas. Distinguished, what? What? Madame Cantelna and her companions from the Soviet Union. From the Soviet Union, Madame Cantelna and her companions. And our young friend, Mr. Rodgers, from the United States of America. From the United States of America, what? What? And we even have a guest here from England. Mr. Anders. From England, what? What? But we're all friends here tonight. All friends here. And all here for the hunting and the merrymaking. The hunting and the merrymaking, what? What? So now I say, what, let us all have a drink and a dance. What? A drink and a dance."

He waved the brush for a third time, and the champagne corks popped like a *feu de joie*. At this signal the orchestra commenced playing; they were tucked away in the gallery which the Wantages usually used as a television room, but which had been restored to its proper function for this night.

"Shall we lead them out?" Dorinda asked Jonathan. "I adore waltzing."

"I'm afraid I'm bespoke," he said, and took Anna's arm.

"Why, Jonathan," she said. "How very charming of you. But surely Dorinda is much more your age group? And far more attractive than I."

"No one could be more attractive than you, Anna." He swung her onto the floor.

"You are sweet," she said. "And you dance very well. Do you remember, Jonathan, how when last we met, on board that ghastly ship, I invited you to accompany me to the Soviet Union? Why did you refuse?"

"I suppose I'm a one-country man."

"An admirable trait. But my offer is still open, you know. You would do very well in the Soviet Union. As I have told you before, we know how to reward talent. And you are a very talented young man."

"Would you say so?"

"I would indeed. You have a tremendous amount of perseverance, which is certainly a talent, and one I will confess I underestimated the last time we met. Not any more. I know now that I will have to be very careful in whatever I try to do, because I am sure that you are going to try to stop me."

"But that doesn't seem to bother you a great deal."

She sighed and dropped her hands as the music ceased. "I suppose I shall have to attempt to outwit you, Jonathan. Although my inclinations are toward doing a deal."

"What sort of a deal?"

"I was thinking of what you said this morning. About having a little chat? Comparing notes, perhaps.

To begin with, I'd like to know if your purpose here is merely to block my endeavors. Or do you wish to obtain Benderer's papers for yourself?"

"Well, both, naturally."

"Jonathan," Dorinda said, joining them as the music started again. "This is a nice and slow and soulful number. Come and dance."

"I'm sorry, darling. I promised Anna this one as well."

She rested her head on his shoulder. "I thought it would be both," she said, and sighed again. "Do you know something, Jonathan? I am growing old. I do not wish to fight, to oppose, to indulge in endless conflict any more. I wish to live at peace, to pursue my experiments. I am a scientist, not a secret agent, and I hate being used as one. I wish to live as friends with everyone. But especially with the British. And most especially with you, Jonathan."

He looked down on that glossy black head, on the soft fingers resting on his own. He remembered that they were also amongst the strongest fingers he had ever encountered. "So?"

"So? So what about that deal, Jonathan? I do not think that even with the help of your American friend you will be able to stop me this time. Last time I was handicapped by a bunch of amateurs. But Tigran and his aides are highly qualified agents of the K.G.B. If you start something, someone is sure to get hurt. I'm sure neither of us really wishes that to happen."

"I'm sure. Go on."

"So therefore I would say that you have no choice but to accept what I am offering, which is this. I will obtain Otto's papers, because I know where they are.

I promise you that. But before I leave for Russia I will let you photograph them. Then both our countries will have equal opportunities for developing his mask, you see? Now, what could be fairer than that?"

It occurred to Jonathan that perhaps Anna Cantelna *was* growing old, and tired. Not in offering him a deal; that was obviously phony. But in assuming that he already knew what he was looking for. Of course it made sense that he should; Anna's handicap was that she didn't know the obscure manner in which Craufurd went about his business. But it was still careless of her. Yet he had to play it very carefully. Too much eagerness on his part might just warn her off.

"How can you be sure the papers are there to be found? Ma Herries denies it."

"Well, of course she would. But she doesn't know the vital point, that Otto and I were friends once. Oh, I was just a girl when he came to Russia. But I was what they call a prodigy, you know, and in my teens I was already at work on marine biology. And Otto, being the leading German in that field, had to be introduced to me. There were even newsreel cameras there, to film the Nazi genius and the Soviet girl prodigy. But do you know what, Jonathan? He liked me. Despite the certainty that before very long we would be on opposite sides, he still liked me. We spent much time talking together, and although he tried to be guarded, yet he was so enthusiastic about his great project he could not help but try to make me understand what he hoped to achieve."

"He was a true scientist," Jonathan said piously. "Oh, darn. The music is stopping again."

"It is a nuisance," she said. "And we cannot be interrupted right this moment. Do you think we could slip away from all these people?"

"Up to the roof, you mean?"

"Brrr. In this rain? This is surely a night for staying indoors. No, no. There are many hiding places in a castle such as this. Lord Wantage very kindly took me on a tour of inspection when we first arrived, and I found it fascinating. Down here." She held his hand and they darted along a little corridor he had not noticed before, leading off the drawing room and giving access to a narrow stone gallery which seemed to extend right round the castle.

"Now we are even outside the bedrooms," she said. "In the old days, there would always be guards here, employed to make sure no one tried to assassinate the lord. Oh, those were tumultuous times. And yet I wonder how the knights of those days would have fared in our own tumults. They would probably all have suffered nervous breakdowns. We go down here."

They had arrived at a flight of steps leading down into the darkness.

"We don't need a light," Anna said. "There are seventeen steps and then another gallery." She still held his hand, tightly. "But I was telling you about dear old Otto. Oh, yes, he was a true scientist, as you say. So enthusiastic about each project it simply wasn't possible to stop talking about it. But you see, it was easy to understand his enthusiasm for Neptune."

"Come again?" Jonathan asked without thinking.

"Ah," Anna said. "You would never have heard

the code title, I suppose. Operation Neptune, he called it. It was, to him, the summit of his achievements, and he had had a brilliant career, as you know. But he had been a U-boat seaman in the First World War, when he had been even younger than you, and very impressionable. He must have seen some horrifying sights. And then he returned to the U-boats the moment Hitler allowed him to. He loved the sea, and particularly the depths of the sea. So what would you expect but that he would make the safety of submariners his life's work?"

They had reached the next floor. Which would be where the guest bedrooms were, Jonathan decided. And still she went on into the darkness. He strained his ears above her soft voice and heard nothing. And yet clearly she was in the very process of making her play. He supposed it was amusing, in a rather gruesome fashion. Anna's sole object was to keep talking so he wouldn't notice what she was doing, where she was taking him. And he had to take the risk just to *keep* her talking, in an effort to find out just what they were both looking for.

"There is another flight here," she said. "Once again, seventeen. The old Normans were certainly methodical. Now, naturally, Otto was fascinated by the dangers of the life. And who can blame him for that either? I can think of no more ghastly way to die than in a submarine trapped on the bottom. I think perhaps Otto really expected to die like that every time he went to sea. Perhaps he even had a wish for it. He regarded life as a personal battle between himself and death, as represented by the waves. And if he could solve the problem of surviving such catastrophes, he felt he would have won, even though he had to die himself, eventually. Because, of course, he had no use for these cumbersome escape devices which rely upon shooting a man upward at tremendous speed; they were slow in loading and required an escape vent. 'No, no, Anna,' he said to me. 'Man can only operate under the sea with impunity if he can turn himself into a fish.' "

"In which idea, of course, he was only anticipating Captain Cousteau," Jonathan said. "Be a bit much, though, to equip every submariner with a couple of lungs. As he realized," he hastily added, and saw light at the foot of the steps, with some relief.

"Of course," Anna agreed. "So here we are in the stables. Hush. Hush," as the hounds started their whining and growling. And remarkably, they did cease their noise. "Would you like to see the dungeons? They are not so romantic as they sound, nowadays. But every castle must have a dungeon."

Here was the crunch, he figured. But he was behind her; just behind her. "Lead on."

"I think, now, we will have lights," she said, to his surprise, and pulled a switch by the stairs. Her behavior was becoming more odd every moment.

"You wouldn't be luring me out of the way while your three friends get on with it, would you?" he asked.

"Now, Jonathan, would I do a thing like that? Would I, indeed, place myself in your power like this? Oh, I well know that you can be as ruthless as anyone, if pushed to it. But we were talking about poor Otto. Of course a lung for every submariner was out of the question. And so limited. But he was never joking, you know. He had no sense of humor. When he said that man must turn himself into a fish, he meant just that. For what is the vital difference between fish and man, when you think about it? Just that mucous membrane in the gills which separates the oxygen from the water. Had man that membrane, he would be no more able to breathe pure air than a goldfish; were he able to assume and discard such a membrane at will, then he would become the first true amphibian. And that was Otto's dream, as you know. Oh, I can see that you remain skeptical. No paper was ever published, and on such an impossible subject no scientist ever expected one. But do you know, our information is that he was on the point of perfecting it when the American bombers struck Oberglattau. A mask, worn over the head and fitting so closely it was to all intents and purposes a second skin, and treated with . . . now there is the question. And Otto's secret. A membrane, so constructed as to act the part of a gill and extract the oxygen from the water, over and over again. Think of it, Jonathan. Think of the possibilities, and not only for submariners, as we now know them. Militarily, for instance, the prospects are endless. For example, your English channel would no longer exist."

"As you said just now, Anna, I'm still a skeptic. But who am I to argue with the powers that be. What puzzles me is how you can be so sure he took his papers out of Oberglattau."

They reached the bottom of the steps. Here the ceiling was much lower, and there was a smell of damp, despite the continuing heat. "This is the well," she said. "All these old towers had their own wells, so that the garrison would always be able to hold out until relieved. You'll see there are no dungeons as such; it's just one big empty space, really. Which is why the towers got their names of donjons, I suppose; just one vast dungeon, from the point of view of the local people. Of course, the boiler wasn't there in the old days. It must have been very unpleasant." She walked farther into the room. "But here, you'll see, are these old rusting chains and collars. Imagine being chained up to one of these, and hearing the servants drawing water, and knowing an entire life was going on above you."

"Gruesome," Jonathan agreed. "You were going to tell me about Otto. Some more about Otto."

"Do come and look at this, Jonathan." She moved even farther into the semidarkness, for the electric light fittings down here were far apart. "This is the rack. Isn't it horrible?"

Jonathan stood beside her, looking down at the two rollers. At this moment it looked innocuous enough.

"Here," Anna said. "Can you see this? Someone has scratched his, or her, initials here. I asked Lord Wantage about it, but he could not tell me whose they are. Can you imagine some poor soul, lying here, waiting to be torn apart, and scratching his initials in the wood?"

"No, I can't," Jonathan said. "Because it isn't possible. Both hands would have been tied. I imagine that's more likely to be the executioner himself."

"Oh, how terrible," she said. "Can you decipher them, Jonathan?"

Jonathan sighed and stood next to the rack, bending forward to peer at the faint marks. "The first one could be a T. But it's difficult to say. And the second looks like a D, I should say."

"Yes," Anna agreed. "I made them that, too. I suppose it means trap door."

Jonathan plunged downward through a tremendous darkness.

PART TWO

THE KILL

CHAPTER 6

Jonathan actually fell only five feet and landed on a soft bottom, composed of what he did not really care to decide. Mud, certainly, and some of the slime which coated the moat, he supposed, covered by enough water to make him as wet as he had been when he returned from the hunt. But the darkness was so intense he found it difficult to breathe for a moment; the trapdoor had already clanged back into place above his head.

"I forgot to mention it." Anna's voice was surprisingly loud and had a hollow quality, suggesting there was some sort of speaking tube leading from the rack into the cell. "But of course there were always two classes of dungeon in these old Norman keeps. One for those who could be described as ordinary malefactors, and a separate black hole for those to whom the baron had actually taken a dislike. And now, I'm afraid you've seen the entire castle, and I must leave you. Jonathan? Jonathan, are you all right?"

Jonathan said nothing. There was always the chance she'd open the trap to make sure. He tensed his muscles for a leap upward should that happen. But Anna, he reflected sadly, did not believe in allowing the opposition chances.

"I am perfectly sure you are all right," she said. "Lord Wantage himself showed me the hole yesterday morning, and there is nothing down there that can injure you. I am going to say good-by for the time being, Jonathan. I do promise you that you will be released in the morning. And for the time being, if you feel like it, you may try shouting. Everyone else in the castle is four floors away, and there is an orchestra playing. So you are unlikely to disturb anyone at all. Oh, and Jonathan, I did understand from the beginning that you had no idea at all about what Otto was working on, but I thought you might like to find out. I also thought it would keep you too interested to worry about other things. And every word I told you about his project was absolutely true. The trouble is, as *no* one has even an inkling as to where Otto's theories even started from—what substance, what chemical, even what experiments—only someone in possession of his own notes could ever possibly hope to follow in his footsteps. So I will say this, if you ever see a monstrous-looking creature walking ashore on any of your English beaches, treat him kindly. He will only be a Russian who will have swum or walked all the way from the Soviet Union."

He heard her heels tapping on the floor for a few seconds, and then there was silence. Not even a drip of water. He was well and truly stuck in. And he had been well and truly dropped in. The plain fact of the matter was that where the last time Anna had been overconfident, considering him as only a boy—and he had perhaps been more afraid of her than he had needed to be—on this occasion he had been the overconfident one. Craufurd had been quite right; he was no detective. Playing one only got him into trouble. Time and again. Where he should have watched and waited, and stayed close to Pete, he had wandered off on his own, and with probably the most dangerous woman in the world.

He had stuck out his chin and said, hit me. And Anna had obliged. Well, who wouldn't?

So there were quite enough recriminations. What happened next? Looking at the worst possible point of view, no one would miss him from the dance before it broke up, and that would be tomorrow morning he suspected. By then Anna would have found her file of papers, or whatever it was she was really looking for, and she would . . . she wouldn't bring it back here, even if she came back here herself to laugh at him. She'd send it on ahead by one of her three pals. By a scheduled flight, of course; she wanted to avoid all possible publicity. That meant Tigran or whoever it was would have to drive down to Shannon, or take the train, and a scheduled flight could not possibly leave before tomorrow morning. That meant there was still time, supposing he could get out of this hole.

He looked up as the trap opened. "I thought you must be down there," Dorinda said, "when it became obvious that you weren't anywhere else."

Jonathan stood up, got his shoulders into the aperture.

"Did Anna push you in?" Dorinda asked innocently.

"I'd suggest you have a good laugh. You could have warned me this castle had trap doors scattered about the floor."

"I never thought of it. And if I had, I'd have decided you deserved whatever you got. Walking around the less-inhabited regions of the castle in the middle of the night with that Russian femme fatale."

"It's not the middle of the night, yet. I hope."

"It soon will be. Aren't you coming out? I think I deserve at least a big kiss for saving you from a most uncomfortable night."

Jonathan got his elbows clear, gave a mighty heave, and sat on the lip beside her.

"On second thought," she said, "I suppose it'll keep. You're *filthy*. You can't possibly come back up to the dance until you've changed."

"I don't think I'll be coming back to the dance, anyway. Where's Anna?"

"Gone."

"How, where, and when?"

"Well, she and her three friends told Papa they wanted to take a drive in the country. They said it was getting too hot and stuffy up there. So he told them to take the Rolls. He's very generous."

"He's also very gullible, if you don't mind my saying so. Drive around the countryside? In the pouring rain? How long ago did they leave?"

"Oh, not more than a few minutes, I think."

He scrambled to his feet. "Then I can still catch them."

"Can you?"

"You have another car, haven't you? What I'd like you to do is nip upstairs and grab Pete. Tell him it's all happening and send him down to the stables."

"But do we *want* to catch up with her?"

"*You* don't have to, Dorinda. But I do. And I may just need Pete."

"At the very least," she agreed. "Are you sure I shouldn't ask . . ."

"Nobody else, if you don't mind. I'm not sure who I can trust around here."

"But you're prepared to trust me? I like that."

"I don't seem to have too much choice. *Will* you get Pete?"

"Oh, all right." She hurried up the stairs. "You go to the car. I'll be right back."

Jonathan nodded, followed her as far as the next level and was greeted with a chorus of barks and whines from the hounds. The gate stood open, and the sports car looked very lonely all by itself. He glanced at his watch; like the rest of him, it was caked in mud and dust. He cleaned the glass, discovered the time was only twenty minutes past six. Still, Anna would be at the inn by now, with no one else in the village at all. It would take her a matter of seconds to break her way in, even supposing Ma Herries had bothered to lock up. Everything now depended on how long it took her to find what she wanted inside.

And what was he going to do about it? Even with Pete beside him? All he could think of at this moment was keeping her under surveillance, harassing her perhaps into making a mistake. At least she'd be surprised, and he hoped, disturbed, to see him again so soon. Anyway, he had no alternatives. If only Craufurd had thought to send along just a little strong arm support.

"I wondered what had happened to you." Pete came running down the stairs, followed by Dorinda, and, unfortunately, by Joan as well. "Dorinda tells me you had a run-in with Anna. In which you didn't do very well."

"Why, Mr. Anders," Joan said. "Sure and ye must have fallen into the moat." She burst into a peal of laughter. "Oh, ye do stink."

"That about sums it up," Jonathan agreed. "Come on, Pete. The little lady has taken herself off. But we can still catch her up. I'll drive."

"You will not." Dorinda had wrapped herself in a mink jacket. "It happens to be my car, and if you don't mind, I'll do the driving."

"Listen, doll, there is just a chance we may be going to get into a spot of bother."

"No one is going to bother me," Dorinda said confidently. "I'm Dorinda Wantage."

"The *Honorable* Dorinda Wantage," Pete reminded her.

"Sure, but where are ye hustling to?" Joan asked.

"The Kiltone Arms, for a start," Jonathan told her.

"Then I'd best come along. It's me own mother's pub," she pointed out.

"This *is* only a two-seater, you know," Dorinda said. "It's going to be a squeeze as it is."

"I think you'd better let us get on with it," Jonathan said. "But the odds are pretty long at the moment. We wouldn't say no to some real assistance. What about Mick and the lads?"

Joan sighed and shook her head. "They'll not lift a finger to help ye."

"Not even to protect your mother's house?" Pete asked.

"Sure and they don't believe a word either of ye are saying about Madame Cantelna. Mick's positive sure that Mr. Anders is here to make trouble for the Army, and is only using the Madame as a cover for his real intentions. If he did come along he'd be far more likely to take ye back into custody than help ye."

"You are a most encouraging soul," Pete said.

"Well, then, maybe the best thing you can do is help us the other way," Jonathan said. "Get back up to the party and stall Mick off if he happens to notice we've left. Will you do that?"

"Sure and I'll try, Mr. Anders." She hesitated, frowning. "They'll be after burgling the house, ye say? And that's where ye'll be going?"

"Yes." Jonathan's turn to frown. "Unless you have any better ideas." He remembered the telephone call he'd asked her to make. "Or any information we could use."

It occurred to him that she did, but she wasn't letting on right this minute. She licked her lips and looked most unhappy. "Sure," she said at last. "Sure and it's the truth I know nothing at all about what ye're at. I'll wish ye luck. And I'll do what I can for ye."

"Good girl," Pete said.

"Well, come *on*." Dorinda was behind the wheel and gunning her engine.

145

Pete climbed into the little space at the back, Jonathan sat beside her; Joan waved, and they clattered across the bridge and went roaring down the drive.

"I've an idea Joan was trying to tell us something," Pete said.

"Same here. But she's your friend. What do you think it was?"

"Only that we're wasting our time in trying the house. Which means that Anna is also."

"Which also means that her Dad's stuff is somewhere else. But she didn't bother to tell us where."

"You were brooding on the caves earlier," Pete said.

Dorinda Wantage swung the small car through the gate on two wheels. Jonathan decided that she wouldn't last all that long at Brands Hatch. He wondered if Joan *had* discovered anything about the Wantages. If she had bothered. But it would make so much difference to know how far Dorinda could be trusted, especially since she had insisted on coming along.

"I thought it was likely, in view of Joan's knowledge of them. Trouble is, Anna hasn't been here long enough to have discovered anything about them, and without knowing her way around she'd hardly risk going in on her own. She didn't take anyone from the village with her, did she, Dorinda?"

"Not that I noticed. So where do you want me to drive?"

"Oh, the house, I suppose," Jonathan said. "We don't have anywhere else to go, and you never know your luck."

"Is that how spies and things work?" she asked with interest, taking a rise in the road at such speed all four wheels left the ground. "Why don't you get out your miniature transmitter and call your boss and ask him what's the best thing to do?"

"Mainly because I don't have a miniature transmitter," Jonathan explained.

"Or a full-sized one, either," Pete said. "Can you really see far enough in this rain? I mean for the speed we're going."

"I know this road like the back of my hand," she said, and wrenched them round the following corner. "Ooops. What's that?"

"Duck!" Jonathan bawled.

The center of the road seemed to be occupied by an enormous stone block, rather like a detached boulder, and too wide to permit a car to pass on either side. Dorinda attempted to swing to the left, where there was less of a parapet falling away from the road itself. But there was too much water accumulated on the tarred surface. The sports car swung round all right, but then the wheels ceased to grip, and it skidded sideways at scarcely any loss of speed. Jonathan saw the stone racing at them, figured this was quite definitely it, and then they slewed into the block with a mighty swoosh. The car seemed to lift and came down again. Its speed was checked as if a giant hand had been stretched out to close on it. Dorinda was thrown away from the wheel and into Jonathan's shoulder; but apart from her scream there was not a sound, except for that of escaping air.

"What on earth . . . ?" Jonathan had to force his

door open against the mound of restraining rubber.

"Rubber!" Pete demanded. "But how the dickens...?"

Jonathan was out of the car, ignoring the rain which poured on his head. "Anchored with six guy ropes, that's how the dickens. Oh, what a cute idea."

"You mean it's just a great balloon?" Dorinda cried.

"That's right. But at night, it certainly looked like an outsize rock."

"You know what saved us?" Pete said. "This blessed rain. If this had not been such a slippery road, we'd have been charging into that field over there, and we'd have had a hard time getting back out."

"We'd never have got back out," Dorinda said somberly. "At least, not with the car. Right over there is one of Kiltone's crazy bogs."

"She meant to stop us all right."

"Or anybody who decided to go home early," Pete suggested.

"You mean Anna planted this?" Dorinda asked.

"Well, who else has passed this road tonight? But it didn't work. Come on."

It took them twenty minutes to pull and drag and tear the cloying rubber away from their wheels and around their bumpers. By then it was absolutely dark.

"You know what?" Pete asked. "She must be carrying a pretty high pressure pump around with her. She only had a half hour start, if that much."

"Which also means she can't be all that far in front of us," Jonathan panted.

"And am I going to have a word or two to say

when we catch up with her," Dorinda muttered. "My dress is absolutely ruined. As for my hair . . ."

"It's coming down," Pete agreed.

"It's come down," Jonathan said. "Shall we get started again?"

They were only a mile from the village now. It lay beneath them, but in contrast to last night it was hardly visible in the rain. A wind arose, whining through the hills and whipping up little catspaws in the sheltered sea loch.

"It's going to be a dirty night," Jonathan remarked.

"You can say that again," Pete agreed.

The car rattled onto the cobbles of the village street.

"Stop here," Jonathan said. "We're making enough noise to wake the dead."

Dorinda braked again, and the car slewed sideways before coming to a halt.

"Do you always stop like that?" Jonathan asked.

"Isn't that what brakes are for? The pub is just down there."

"We know. Come on."

Jonathan ran down the deserted street, reached the swinging sign. The door was locked.

"Well, anyway, they'd hardly just bust the front door lock and walk in," Pete argued.

"I don't even know how you get round the back," Jonathan admitted.

"Through here." Dorinda dragged dripping hair from her eyes, plastered it to her head, and led them through a narrow alleyway between the inn and the cottage next door. Something moved away from their feet with a hiss. "Oh, Lord! What's that?"

"Just a cat," Jonathan reassured her. "Here's another door."

"And it's locked, too," Dorinda wailed.

"But this fence is only seven feet or so high," Pete said. "Give me a boost, Jon."

Jonathan made a back, and Pete went up in a single bound, sat astride for a moment, and dropped to the other side with a splash. "Oops! Seems there's not too much drainage back here."

"Shall we come over?" Jonathan asked.

"No. Just a moment while I have a look around. But I don't think there's anyone here."

They heard a few more splashes, and then silence. Dorinda hugged herself. "Do you know I'm soaked to the skin? And my mink is going to be ruined. It's only a year old. Is spying always like this?"

"It has its uncomfortable moments," Jonathan agreed. "I thought you weren't going to become involved?"

"I'm not. Except in this beastly rain. I'm acting as your chauffeuse, remember? Don't count on me if any rough stuff develops, because then I'll be off home."

"I'll bear that in mind. Is that you, Pete?"

There was a scrabbling sound beyond the wall. "Yeah," Pete gasped, and got his head over the top. He pulled himself up until he could sit astride, looked down on them. "There's not a sign or a squeak of a single living soul over here."

"They'll have heard us coming and be lying low," Dorinda suggested.

"Where, for instance?" Pete demanded. "There's no sign of any forced entry back here. You know what I think? I think we boobed. They didn't come here at all."

"But they came in this direction," Jonathan said. "Else why go to all that trouble to block the road? And Anna said quite definitely that she knew where to look . . ."

"So they've come and gone, maybe," Dorinda suggested. "Had a look and found nothing. Even Anna Cantelna *can* be wrong, you know. Maybe Mr. Herries really didn't leave anything."

"I hate to keep repeating this," Pete said, "but nobody has broken into this inn tonight."

"Hey," Jonathan said. "Of course they didn't break in here. They weren't coming to the inn at all. I've just remembered. That's exactly what Ma Herries said last night when I was talking with her in the bar. She was quite amused about it. She said, 'George didn't *leave* anything behind, Mr. Anders.' Exactly what Dorinda just said."

"Oh, great," Dorinda said. "So he took it with him. Up or down, do you think?"

"Six feet down," Jonathan said.

"Of course," Pete shouted. "They weren't trying to put the old lady off. They offered her cash to be allowed to photograph her husband in his coffin."

"Ugh!" Dorinda said. "What a morbid lot."

"But don't you see," Pete said. "They're not interested in old George. But in what he has on him. He must've left instructions to have his papers buried with him . . ."

"And digging up a grave is quite a business in a

small community like this," Jonathan said. "So Anna tried to do it legitimately first."

"And when that didn't work," Pete said, "she had to wait for a change in the weather. Last night the moon was just too bright to risk anything. So *that's* what Tigran meant when he said this was going to be a good day. And that explains everything that's been bothering us about this whole setup."

"So let's go," Jonathan said.

"To the cemetery?" Dorinda asked. "Oh, brother. I'll get the car."

"We'll go on foot," Jonathan said. "Body snatching is something you want to do quietly."

"But it's nearly half a mile," Dorinda wailed. "Way over on the other side of the village."

"We know." Jonathan took her elbow. "We passed it last night."

"And in this rain," she grumbled. "Anyway, I'd rather go in the car. It can travel faster than I can run."

"You won't be running anywhere," Jonathan promised her. "Now let's get on with it."

They splashed their way down the street, staying close to the houses, although there was not much risk of them being heard by anyone. The rain was, if anything, falling harder now than at any moment of the day. At the last house they paused and huddled close together, because out here they were exposed to the brisk wind coming up from the Atlantic. In front of them the church was a dark shadow, perhaps four hundred yards away.

"I don't see anything at all," Pete whispered.

"Look over there." Jonathan pointed to where the road dwindled into the path which eventually led up the hill; the path Joan Herries had followed the previous night. At the end of the road there was a large black shadow.

"Papa's car," Dorinda breathed.

"So we know we're on the right track," Jonathan said. "Now you two wait here."

He bent double, ran across the open space as fast as he could, squelching ankle deep in the soft wet grass; after what seemed an eternity he gained the gravel path which led up to the door of the church itself. A moment later he was in the shelter of the building, leaning against the wet stone wall and gasping as if he'd just run five miles. He waited a moment to let his breathing settle down, then inched his way along the building to the buttress and looked round it. The cemetery itself was immediately in front of him now, and somewhat below the church itself, which enabled him to see the Russian party. Two were digging, and another smaller one was standing behind them, looking on, hands thrust deep into her coat pocket. That had to be Anna. So where was the third man? But it was so dark, and the tall gravestones created so many additional darknesses that he could be anywhere.

Jonathan ran back along the wall and waved his arm. Dorinda came across next, slipped in the mud, and fell flat on her face. Pete followed, pulled her back to her feet, and pushed her onto the gravel.

"Oh, lord!" she gasped as she came into the shelter of the church. "I'm simply covered in mud. Look at my hands."

"It's your face I'm interested in," Jonathan said. "You could be a commando. But it's a very good camouflage. Now listen. They're there, all right. I'm going to try to get up closer, and see, or hear, what they find. You two stay here."

"Now you listen," Pete said.

"I'm not cutting you out of any action," Jonathan promised. "You can see what's going on from that buttress over there. But it stands to reason that one of us stands a better chance of getting up close than all three. If I need you, I'll shout."

"You better," Pete said.

"And Jonathan..." Dorinda hesitated. "Be careful. I suppose they *could* be armed."

He grinned at her. "It's just possible. But Russians are notoriously bad shots. See you in church."

He left the shelter of the wall, crossed the lawn which adjoined it, and ducked through the gate to the cemetery, which Anna had fortunately left open. Now he was in the midst of the gravestones, and once again on gravel, which scuffed beneath his feet. He bent double, crept from stone to stone, and reached a large monument close to the place where George Herries had been buried. Anna had sat down on another stone by now, her raincoat wrapped around her, legs crossed, patiently watching her two assistants, who worked with great method, digging their spades in, one on each side, and tossing out the mud. Jonathan figured they still had some way to go.

He wondered if there was any means of approaching closer, looked around him, and decided against it. Here he could see everything that was going on, and there was little risk of his own whereabouts being discovered. But what would happen when they were finished? He could only hope that they *would* then split up, send one man on with the papers while the others returned to Kiltone Castle.

One of the digging men, Ewfim he thought, said something, and Anna nodded. The two Russians were almost waist deep in the soft ground by now, and presumably were close to the top of the casket. Jonathan shivered, but that surely was because of the rain which was completely soaking his clothing. He might as well be wearing a bathing suit, he thought ruefully.

He watched Anna get up, switch on a flashlight, walk to the edge of the grave and look down. She then turned, with a sharpness which made his heart bound as he followed the direction of her gaze.

Three figures came down the central path. Dorinda walked first, her hands clasped on her neck. Pete followed, also with his hands raised. And behind them both walked Tigran carrying in his right hand a large automatic pistol.

"Tigran?" Anna demanded in Russian. "What has happened?"

Tigran replied, also in Russian, but speaking too quickly for Jonathan to understand. Dorinda was also apparently not satisfied.

"Pete and I were taking a little rainy drive," she said. "Just like you, Anna. And Pete wanted to see the old church. So we got out to take a look, and I slipped and fell. We were just trying to go back to the car when this great gorilla comes along and waves a gun at us. Look at my dress, Anna. It's absolutely ruined. If it shrinks, I've a good mind to send you the bill. As for my coat . . ."

"Be quiet, you silly girl," Anna said, more sharply than Jonathan had heard her speak for a long time. "Where is Jonathan?"

"She's telling the truth, you know," Pete said. "We were out for a quiet spin. Now why on earth should we have Jon along? Don't they have that old saying in the Soviet Union, two's company, three's a crowd?"

"My dear Mr. Rodgers," Anna said. "To this moment I have credited you with a great deal of intelligence. Please now prove me right by, in turn, crediting me with at least a little. Tigran has been watching you since you entered the village. He made no move to interfere with you while you were worrying about the public house, and afterward he unfortunately had to stay rather farther back than he would have liked. But he saw the three of you go into the shelter of the church. Now there are only two of you. So where is Mr. Anders at this moment?"

"Why don't you get lost?" Dorinda asked.

Anna gave an order in Russian, and the other two men stopped digging. They threw their spades to the ground and crawled out of the hole with much grunting and puffing.

"Now," Anna said. "Hold Mr. Rodgers."

"Hey, wait a moment," Pete said, but each had already seized an arm, and he was helpless.

"You get down into that pit, Dorinda," Anna commanded.

"You have got to be joking," Dorinda remarked. "I'm getting the willies just standing here. I didn't know you people went in for grave robbing, Anna."

Anna glanced at Tigran, who promptly pocketed

the pistol and seized Dorinda by the shoulders. She tried to kick him on the shin, but he merely sidestepped, grabbed her round the waist instead, and lifted her off her feet.

"Anna!" Dorinda wailed. "I'm Dorinda Wantage."

"Listen to me," Anna said, speaking in a low voice, but so clearly that Jonathan could hear every word, even above the rain. "You think I am joking with you? The time for joking is past. I have a job of work to do now, and I will do it, regardless of who has to get hurt. You will call out and tell Jonathan to join us. I know he is around here, and I also know that he is not armed. Your own servant, Clay, found that out for me, did he not? Whereas all four of us are armed."

Tigran set Dorinda back on her feet, but retained hold of her arms. She gave him an angry look, and then turned back to Anna. "I thought you were my friend," she said. "Or Papa's friend, anyway."

"And no doubt I shall be your friend again, if you will do as I say and stop being a little idiot. And if I try very hard to swallow my natural instincts. Now call out to your friend Jonathan."

Dorinda's chin came up. "And suppose I won't? It wouldn't do any good, anyway. If you must know the truth, Jonathan left the two of us at the church to keep an eye on you while he went off to raise the rest of his group. He's not alone, you know. Oh, no, no, no. He's just here to get you to show your hand, as you're doing now, and then he'll have a dozen British agents on top of you. You're going to go to prison, all of you."

"And I thought you were a sensible child," Anna

said. "Can you not realize that Jonathan and I are professionals? We have met before in this business. We know each other very well. We know each other's methods. And I know he is always alone." She shrugged. "Very well. Get down into that grave."

"I won't." Dorinda's voice quavered.

Anna nodded to Tigran, and the big man swept Dorinda from her feet once again.

"Let me go!" she screamed, but she was already at the lip of the grave, and a moment later disappeared from sight. "Ooh!" she screamed. "You . . ."

"You can start filling it in, Vassily," Anna said. "Give him a hand, Ewfim. Your gun, Tigran? He will shoot you, Mr. Rodgers, if you attempt to move."

"You . . ." Dorinda screamed.

"After all, Dorinda," Anna said, "when one has an open grave, it would be stupid not to use it, wouldn't you say?"

Vassily dug his spade into the freshly turned earth, threw it into the pit.

"Oh!" Dorinda shouted. "That went right down my neck. You . . ."

"It won't take very long," Anna promised. "With the earth this soft and wet, suffocation will occur in a few seconds after you are totally covered."

"Oh!" Dorinda wailed.

"Now say, wait a moment," Pete said.

"You be quiet, Mr. Rodgers. Your turn will come soon enough."

Ewfim dumped his spadeload in. "Oh, lord!" Dorinda moaned. "Jonathan! ! ! !"

Jonathan chewed his lip. Of course Anna was

not really going to bury her alive; she hadn't taken out Otto Benderer's casket yet, and there was no point in making her men do the work twice. But she was quite capable of terrifying the poor girl right out of her wits.

He stood up. "Hello, Anna. Wet, what?"

"Jonathan!" Dorinda screamed. "Oh, Jonathan, get me out of here."

"Jonathan," Anna said with less emotion. "Do you know, I had overlooked the possibility that this young woman might succeed in developing a crush on you? Had I realized that, I'd have locked the pair of you up together. Then we wouldn't have been interrupted at all. But I am interested to know what you made of our little toy."

"I'd have thought you were a bit old to play with balloons, Anna. If you must know, we drove right through it. Write it off as a failure."

"I had my doubts, Tigran," she agreed. "Ah, well. Now that you are here you can join her in the hole. You too, Mr. Rodgers."

"But I want to come out," Dorinda wailed. "It's all wet and horrible down here. And I think I'm standing on a coffin. I want to come out. Help me out, Jonathan. I want to go home."

"You will come out as soon as the coffin is uncovered," Anna said. "So if you really wish to do her a favor, Jonathan, I suggest you start digging, to the best of your ability. You too, Mr. Rodgers."

Jonathan shrugged. "May as well humor her, Pete. She's holding all the high cards while Tigran here has his howitzer." He slid down the slope, joined

Dorinda at the bottom. They were definitely standing on wood rather than earth; his feet made a hollow thud.

"It *is* a coffin," Dorinda squealed, and threw both arms round his neck. "Oh, Jonathan, I didn't want to become involved. I told you that."

Anna stood above them. "I can believe that, Dorinda. You and your father make me perfectly ill, even to think about. Let me tell you, child, the world is too small for opting out. We are all involved in everything that happens."

"John Donne," Jonathan said.

"What do you mean?"

"He said the very same thing, oh, four hundred years ago. I suppose nothing ever really changes. You remember it, Anna? 'Never send to know for whom the bell tolls; it tolls for thee.' Hemingway used it as a title for a book."

"You are quite a scholar, Jonathan," Anna said. "Now would you mind starting work? We do not have all the night."

Jonathan sighed and dug his spade into the soft earth. Pete followed his example.

"There are three spades, Dorinda," Anna said.

"But I don't know how to use one," Dorinda complained. "I'm not a gardener."

"Then learn. Watch your boyfriend."

"Just dig it in like this," Jonathan told her.

"Oof!" She obeyed, nearly fell over. "Now I'm standing on my skirt. I'm sure it tore then. Did you hear it tear, Jonathan? Oh, when I get out of here . . ."

"You won't at all if you don't shut up and dig," Pete pointed out.

It took them ten minutes' hard labor to uncover the lid of the coffin.

"That will do," Anna said. "There really is no need to go to all of the trouble of bringing it up." She switched on her flashlight once again, shone it into the hole. "Now use your spades, Jonathan, and you, Mr. Rodgers, to break those locks. We want that lid up. Quickly, now."

"Ye'll do no such thing," Joan Herries said. "And ye'll just put away that pistol, Mr. Tigran, and raise your hands in the air."

CHAPTER 7

"Sure and ye're entirely surrounded," Pat O'Rourke said as Tigran showed some hesitation.

They now both came close enough to be seen; Anna turned her light upon them.

"Well, glory be, Joan," Pete said. "I always thought you were the prettiest thing in all Ireland."

"You mean you actually persuaded Mick to cooperate?" Jonathan asked. "Well, good for you. And for him."

Anna Cantelna sighed. "You'd better put away your pistol, Tigran," she said. "These Irishmen are very liable to start shooting."

"He'll drop it on the ground," Joan insisted. "That way we'll know ye can't change your mind."

Tigran hesitated, and then dropped the gun into the mud with a squelch.

"They're all armed," Jonathan said.

"Well, then, ye'd best all disarm," Joan commanded.

Anna bit her lip, but she took a small automatic

pistol from her coat pocket and dropped it in the mud. Ewfim and Vassily followed her lead; their pistols were considerably larger.

"Sure and there's enough fire power to start a war," Pat remarked.

"Will you *please* get me out of here?" Dorinda begged. "I'm just never going to be the same."

Pete was already climbing out of the hole. Jonathan scooped Dorinda round the thighs and lifted her up, and Pete took her hands and pulled her clear. Jonathan followed.

"Now look here," Anna said. "I'm sure we can come to some arrangement, Miss Herries. The fact is, in case you don't understand it, that Jonathan here, and Mr. Rodgers, both want to have a look at your father's papers just as much as I. Now supposing you let us finish what we came for, and then we can all take photographs of the paper, and then, if you like, you can bury your father all over again. Isn't that fair?"

"No one disturbs me dad," Joan said. "Not now he's finally gone to his rest. And that's final."

"But his experiments could prove to be of inestimable value to humanity," Anna said.

"Then ye go ahead and reinvent them," Joan said. "Now be off with ye, all the four of ye. Take the Rolls and get back up to the castle. We don't want to see ye in Kiltone again."

"What about us?" Jonathan asked.

"Whisht," she said. "Ye'll stay here, of course, until the Russians have gone."

"At the very least," Pat said.

"Now I know you're joking," Jonathan said. "If

you don't mind, we'll leave as well. I don't want you to think for one moment that we're ungrateful. But I'm not very keen on being exposed to Mick and the boys for too long either."

"Ah, sure and ye'll be all right," Joan said.

Anna Cantelna switched off her flashlight. "I think," she said, "before I leave, I'd like a word with Mick. And the boys. They are all around us, did you say?"

"All around," Pat said.

"Would you ask Mick to show himself?"

"Sure and he'll do no such thing," Joan said. "But he's a mighty impatient man, Mick is, Miss Cantelna. Ye'd best be away."

"And I am an impatient woman, Miss Herries. Pick up your gun, Tigran. These young women are playing some sort of a game."

"Get him," Jonathan yelled, and dived at Tigran himself. He struck the big man on the shoulder, bowled him over, and they collapsed together on the wet ground. Pete ran forward to reach the gun, and was in turn attacked by Anna, who fell over and threw both arms round his waist. He lost his footing and slipped to the earth. Joan grasped Anna and dragged her away, was in turn knocked down by Vassily, who immediately found himself grappling with Pat. Dorinda gathered her mud-soaked skirt in one hand and tried to run for the gravel path, but Ewfim was too quick for her. He threw himself full length and brought her down with a football tackle. She turned round and hit him twice on the head, but he did not let go.

Jonathan and Tigran rose together, and Jonathan closed his fist and drove it into the Russian's midriff. But Tigran was wearing a topcoat over his dinner jacket and scarcely seemed to feel the punch at all. He clamped his hands on Jonathan's throat, and desperately Jonathan clasped both hands together and brought them down on the Russian's neck, where it joined his shoulders. Tigran grunted and began worrying him—like a dog might worry a rat, still holding him by the throat and shaking him to and fro. Jonathan saw stars blazing across the darkness in front of his eyes and rolled himself backward, knees coming up into Tigran's stomach. It was a good throw; Tigran sailed over his head and lost his grip. Jonathan turned on his knees and was struck from behind by what he assumed must be the blunt end of a pistol. For a moment the stars were back and twice as numerous, and he thought he lost consciousness. He was next aware of lying face down in the mud while someone gently kicked him in the ribs.

"I'm sorry I had to hit you, Jonathan, really I am," Anna Cantelna said. "But I have to admit that for a moment there I almost lost my temper. If there is one thing I hate, it is interference by amateurs."

He sat up and rubbed the back of his head. Anna had switched on her light again and illuminated a scene of absolute disaster, from his point of view. Tigran was just getting to his feet. Vassily stood above Pete, who was also looking a little dazed as he cleaned mud from his glasses. Joan and Pat were disentangling themselves from each other and from the mud. Ewfim had made Dorinda sit down, and stood next to her, ready to join in the next round should it become necessary. But Anna, with only the knees of her green pants suit mud-stained, in complete contrast to everyone else, had regained possession of her pistol.

Joan rubbed mud from her eyes. "I'm sorry, Pete. I'm sorry, Mr. Anders. I really thought we'd get away with it. If only ye hadn't started arguing."

"So where are your gentleman friends?" Anna asked.

"Still at the dance, I suppose," Pat said disconsolately. "We came down in Paddy's horse and trap."

"Well," Anna said. "I think we should get on with what we were doing before that senseless interruption. Dorinda? Are you capable of doing some more digging?"

"Oh, leave me alone," Dorinda wailed. "My dress is torn, my hair is ruined, I've lost one of my shoes, and I think I've swallowed some mud."

"And you will surely catch a cold if you continue to sit on that wet grass. You, too, Mr. Rodgers. Up you get, Jonathan, I think we will keep you and your friends where I can see you. Vassily, they will not be giving us any more trouble right this moment. Get down into that grave and open up the casket. Quickly, now."

"But there's nothing there," Joan cried. "Please believe me."

"I would have supposed you'd understand by now that I am not to be bluffed," Anna said. "You do not seem to realize that I knew your father quite well once upon a time. When I asked him who was helping him in his work, who would carry on with it after he died, he told me that he worked alone, using only laboratory assistants, allowing no one to know what he actually intended. I think the truth of the matter is that when he was a young man, a senior colleague stole some of his notes and put them forward as his own creations, and Otto never forgave either the man in particular or mankind in general. It was a serious flaw in an otherwise brilliant personality.

"But suppose you died, I asked him? And he laughed and said, 'Then my experiment dies with me. Why should anyone else ever get the credit for my years of work? When I die, my papers will go into my grave with me. I have written it into my will.' Oh, he was a strange man. A selfish genius, when it came to his work; the most charming and generous of men in his private affairs. And if I ever had any doubts, they are now gone, because George Herries was buried with papers in his pocket. Tigran here discovered that from the undertaker in Sligo."

"There's nothing there," Joan obstinately repeated. "I'm telling ye, Miss Cantelna. Sure, Dad was laid out by them men from Sligo, and the papers were there then. But I took them away. Don't ye think he remembered what he'd told ye, and what he had always boasted about? But he'd changed his mind before he died. Living here, in Kiltone, with the fisherfolk, watching the sea every day, and growing old, he'd gone back to what he really was, a sailor. And sailors help sailors, whether they're on top of the waves or underneath. He never told me mother what he was thinking, but he told me. He and I were friends, not just father and daughter. 'Ye watch, Joannie,' he told me. 'When they discover who's buried in that coffin, they'll be around as thick as flies. Russians,' he said. 'They'll be here first. But the

British and the Americans won't be far behind.' Oh, he knew exactly what was going to happen. 'So ye let them get on with it, Joannie,' he said. 'But ye'll take the papers from my pocket before they bury me, and ye'll put them where I told ye.' And I did that."

"Did you indeed," Anna remarked. "And now you are going against his last wishes by spoiling his fun, as he called it? I find that difficult to believe."

"Sure, well, it's not right to disturb the dead," Joan said. "He didn't care. He didn't believe in anything. And I never really thought it would come to this. But it isn't right."

"I know," Anna said sadly. "It is a tragic world, this one in which we live. But you do not seriously expect me to believe you? Now, I will have no more delays. Jonathan, you stand over there with the young ladies and Mr. Rodgers. And pleased be assured, both of you, that as it is I who is now holding the pistol, I will shoot you down without the slightest hesitation if you so much as scratch your head. Over you go now."

Jonathan helped Dorinda to her feet.

"Oh!" she said. "How I ever allowed you to get me mixed up in anything like this I shall never know. I'm never going to be clean again. As for this dress, it's only fit for the rubbish bin. And my mink . . ."

"Think of all the memories you'll have," Jonathan suggested. "This is one first day of the Hunt you'll never forget."

"Sure and I'm sorry it turned out this way, Mr. Rodgers," Joan said again. "I couldn't think of any other way to help ye."

"And you tried, that's the essential thing," Pete

agreed. "Besides, I thought you were going to call me Pete, remember?"

"Now, Vassily," Anna said. "A few blows from the spade should smash those locks. Have you got a light? Tigran, shine the other flashlight into the grave." She herself kept her own light playing over her five prisoners. And Jonathan felt absolutely no inclination to take risks with Anna's finger round the trigger.

Vassily's shoulders appeared above the grave, the spade arcing around his head, and there was a clang, and then another.

"Sure and it was such a lovely coffin," Pat said sadly.

Two more clangs, and Vassily grunted with satisfaction.

"Well, then, please hurry," Anna said.

Vassily attacked the coffin once again, and the clangs became regular. But it did not take him very long to shout something triumphantly in Russian.

"You will go down and assist him, Ewfim," Anna said. "Stay with the light, Tigran. The paper we wish will be in his inside breast pocket, I imagine, but if not, try the others." She smiled at Joan. "Would you care to look at your father for a last time? After all, he has been dead less than a week. He will still be quite recognizable."

Joan made no reply.

"You are a perfectly horrible woman, Anna," Jonathan said. "You can be."

"Because I am a realist, Jonathan?" she asked. "And not a romantic? Why does death, the thought of death, upset all of you Westerners so terribly much?

169

Do you believe in your various religions? Whatever they may be? Then surely you must feel that Otto is now a very happy man. He has nothing with which to reproach himself in life. He worked for the good of mankind, in the main. He cannot be condemned out of hand simply because he once commanded a U-boat. Does everyone who has ever been a soldier or a sailor or an airman go straight to hell? Well, then, it must be a grossly overcrowded place.

"And if you do not believe in any soul or any afterlife, then he was a creature who lived and breathed and loved and enjoyed himself while he was alive, like the rest of us. He, in fact, enjoyed life more and lived longer than most of us, and he is now dead. As will we all be dead one day. Dead, he feels nothing, knows nothing, cares nothing. Dead, he is no longer of any importance in this world. Dead, he interests us only for whatever of value he has left behind him. There is your true immortality, Jonathan. Your only immortality. Whatever of value you leave behind when you die. In that respect, Otto is going to be immortal, because he assured that I will give his name full credit for the mask when I have developed it. I do not need any additional fame. Now, Miss Herries, does that not please you? Leave your father down there in that grave, untouched, and he will be forgotten in a month. I am trying to assure him of everlasting fame. I am doing him the greatest honor one can do any man. And you object. In any event, if I may remind you of your own words, he expected his coffin to be opened or he would not have given you those instructions you claim to have received. Well, Vassily?"

Vassily muttered in Russian. Whatever Anna's reasoning, he was not enjoying his work.

"What do you mean?" Anna snapped. "Try the other pockets."

Vassily muttered again.

"There's nothing there I tell ye," Joan whispered. "And may ye rot in hell for this, Miss Cantelna."

Anna gazed at her for several seconds. "Well, Vassily?" she asked again.

"*Nyet,*" Vassily said, and climbed out of the grave. The rain was still falling steadily, yet he took his handkerchief from his pocket to wipe his face.

"All right," Anna said. "Ewfim, replace the lid."

There was another dull thud as Ewfim hurriedly obeyed.

"All right, Miss Herries," Anna said. "Or perhaps I should start calling you Fräulein Benderer, as you so faithfully obeyed your father's instructions. Tell us where you have concealed his papers."

"I'll see ye in jail first," Joan said in a low voice. "And I *will* see ye in jail, Miss Cantelna."

"You are a very stupid girl, Fräulein," Anna said. "Did you not hear what I was saying just now? Would you deny your father immortality?"

"He'll have immortality," Joan said. "Every kind of immortality. Why d'ye think he gave me the papers? To pass on to whomever I thought fit. He said I'd know, when the time came."

"And you do not consider that the time has come as yet?"

Joan glanced at Pete Rodgers. "No," she said. "Not quite."

"Ah," Anna said. "So that is the direction in which the wind is blowing. Very well." Suddenly her voice took on a snap. "You. Your name is Patricia, isn't it?" She pointed with her pistol. "Get down into that grave."

"Me?" Pat cried. "Ye must be daft."

"Vassily, tie her hands together," Anna said. She never took her gaze from the five young people in front of her, and the beam of the flashlight never wavered an inch. "I'll kill you, Jonathan, if you so much as move a muscle. You too, Mr. Rodgers. Please be certain about that."

Vassily took a length of cord from his coat pocket and tied Pat's hands together in front of her.

"She made me go down there," Dorinda remarked, unhelpfully. "It was ghastly."

"Joannie! ! ! ?" Pat wailed.

"What are ye meaning to do?" Joan asked.

"I am going to endeavor to force you to tell me where you hid your father's papers, Fräulein Benderer," Anna said. "And having an open grave, it seems a pity to waste it. As Dorinda says, it persuaded these other three idiots to behave themselves. Is the coffin lid in place, Ewfim?"

The Russian nodded.

"Then come out here. Now, Vassily, will you persuade this young woman to get down."

"No!" Pat shouted. "No. I'll not go in there." She attempted to dig her feet into the soft mud, but Vassily picked her up as easily as if she had been a small child, walked to the edge of the grave, and dropped her in.

"Joannie!" she screamed. "Joannie! Help me!"

Joan chewed her lip while Jonathan tensed his muscles. He did not doubt that this time Anna meant every word she said; he had never seen her so angry. In which case he was about to be shot. Because he couldn't just stand by and watch a young girl killed in the most horrible possible manner.

"Now, Ewfim and you, Vassily, you may fill in the grave," Anna commanded.

The two men picked up their spades.

"Joannie ! ! !" Pat bawled. But they could not see her head; she was too small, even when presumably standing up.

Jonathan glanced at Pete. When he went, he did not doubt that Pete would come behind. But he'd stop the first bullet.

"Wait," Joan said. "All right, Miss Cantelna. Ye've got us where ye want us, for the time being. I'll take ye to the papers."

"Take me?"

"Sure and ye'll never get there by yourself," Joan pointed out. "But where I go, so does Pat. And me other friends."

Anna nodded. "All right. We'll all go. Jonathan, you and Mr. Rodgers may assist that girl from the pit, and then you can fill it in." She looked at her watch. "It's getting on for nine o'clock. Do you realize I have been here over two hours? I'm sure we are all very wet and cold and tired. Unnecessarily so. The sooner we are out of this rain the better."

"Sure and ye soon will be," Joan promised.

Jonathan climbed down into the grave, put his

arm round Pat's shoulders. "Take it easy now," he told the shivering girl. "Nothing is going to happen to you."

"Don't untie her wrists, Jonathan," Anna said. "Pass her up as she is."

Jonathan gave her a boost, and Pete held her arms and pulled her out.

"Now come along, Jonathan," Anna said impatiently. "Grab a spade and fill it in. You too, Mr. Rodgers. Ewfim, give them a hand. We do not want to leave all this mess behind to show what we have been doing. I'm sure it would upset the villagers in the morning. Now you may tell me where we are going from here, Fräulein Benderer."

"Sure and we're trying to climb that hill over there," Joan said. "The papers ye want are in those caves."

"You were right after all, Jonathan." Pete ladled earth into the grave.

"Caves?" Anna asked. "I see no caves."

"They're there," Joan promised her. "Old smugglers' caves. Me dad found them one day when he was walking along the clifftop. Oh, some of the villagers knew they were there, but they never went down. They're supposed to be haunted, and that, with the ghost of some smuggler who was trapped by the tide. But Dad explored them from beginning to end. And when I was a girl he took me with him. Sure and there's miles and miles of them. And I am the only person left who knows them all."

Jonathan sighed with relief as he began stamping down the earth. She hadn't mentioned Mick and the rifles, which meant that she hadn't lost her head. Which also meant that there was still a lot of play left in this game.

"How interesting," Anna said. "Well, I look forward to seeing these caves of yours. But I rather suspect from your tone that you have some idea of perhaps playing us a trick when you have got us down into there. We shall have to take precautions against that. Vassily, you will tie all of their wrists. You have sufficient cord with you?"

Vassily nodded.

"Now really, Anna," Dorinda complained. "How are we going to climb that hill with our hands tied?"

"And in evening dress, too," Anna said sympathetically. "But I'm sure Tigran will be prepared to help you. Are you finished, Jonathan? Your wrists, please."

Jonathan hesitated. With every moment she was taking more and more command of the situation, and of everyone present. But with four pistols knocking about, what *could* he do? Oh, that old blighter. If he only was allowed some weapon of his own other than his brain.

"Jonathan!" Anna's tone was brittle.

He held out his wrists, and Vassily secured them. Then it was Pete's turn. The Russians had already bound the other two girls.

"Good," Anna said. "Now, let us hurry. You will go first, Fräulein, with your little friend beside you. Then, if anything goes wrong, I can shoot her and you will still be alive to take us where we wish to go. So I am third. Jonathan, you will come behind me,

175

and Vassily, you will walk behind Mr. Anders. Do not hesitate to shoot him if he makes any move you dislike. Mr. Rodgers, you will follow Vassily, and Ewfim, you will come behind Mr. Rodgers. My instructions to you are the same. Dorinda, you will come behind Ewfim, and Tigran, you will be our rear guard. There will be no necessity to shoot Miss Wantage, as, after all, we have enjoyed her father's hospitality. You may hit her on the head should she attempt to misbehave, and you will, of course, support Ewfim and Vassily should it become necessary. You will carry the other flashlight. Shall we go?"

She had a mind like a razor, Jonathan remembered ruefully. She never missed a trick, and he did not really see how her dispositions could either be improved or faulted. Any attempt on his part to grapple with her would only cost Pat a bullet in the back and earn himself one as well. Even supposing, with his hands tied together, he could possibly be a match for Anna; he remembered that she knew a lot about unarmed combat.

So what was to be done now? He did not think that Joan would try any more tricks for a while. He thought that she would probably take them directly to where she had hidden her father's papers; it was certain to be in one of the more inaccessible passageways in the entire network. But after that, what did she have in mind? An attempt to lose Anna in the darkness of the passageways, which he remembered only too well? In which case, if she was going to accomplish that, she'd have to lose them all. And if she did that, it was going to be a long night. Even if she meant to come back for them later, it would certainly be with Mick and his friends.

And what about Otto Benderer's notes? He was still on a job. He couldn't admit that he was licked. He had to find some way of getting his hands free, of getting Anna away from her three supporters, and of getting Anna's gun away from her.

As he had supposed, it was going to be a long night.

They filed past the Rolls Royce, waiting wetly in the rain, and reached the foot of the cliff path. They climbed. The ground was soft, and the rain continued to teem down; they slipped and staggered, and the prisoners often fell, trying to catch themselves on their bound hands and being pulled back to their feet by the person behind. Dorinda began to weep with distress, but Tigran resolutely forced her onward. They reached the top after what seemed to be a long eternity, and Jonathan estimated that he was possibly more wet from sweat than from rain.

"What a steep climb," Anna panted. "We will rest for a minute." She turned round to smile at Jonathan, and instead looked past him. "What is that light?"

They all turned, watched the twin ribbons of light coming slowly over the brow of the hill on which stood Kiltone Castle.

"Sure and that's Tim's taxi," Joan said. "It has to be. There isn't any other motor car in Kiltone."

"Good old Tim," Pat said. "I'll bet he has the boys with him."

"The boys?" Anna asked. "Oh, you mean the

young men who were supposed to be surrounding us. The same ones who were at the castle? Rather a harmless-looking lot, I thought. Do you think they are searching for you. Fräulein? Perhaps you are hoping they will follow us up here."

"They may turn out to be slightly tougher than you imagine," Jonathan remarked. "Those harmless-looking characters are all fighting members of the Irish Republican Army, Anna. You don't want to let any of them draw a bead on you, whether it's a rifle or a gasoline bomb." What a crazy, mixed-up world it is, he thought, that a British agent should actually be glad to see a carload of I.R.A. trigger-happies on the way.

"Hmm," Anna said. "You have not answered my question, Fräulein Benderer."

"They're not looking for us," Joan said. "Ye can be sure of that."

"Then tell me why they should have left the entertainment this early? I was informed by Lord Wantage that his dances on the first night of the Hunt usually last until dawn."

"Maybe this one has turned out to be a flop," Pete suggested.

"Sure and they'll have missed these two gentlemen," Pat suggested.

"On the other hand, they're hardly likely to start looking for the pair of them up here," Anna suggested.

"They're not interested in any of us, Anna," Jonathan said. "Except insofar as we might get in their way. If you want the truth, they're on their way to move a shipload of rifles and ammunition they brought in last night. And do you know where the stuff is hidden? Right in the middle of those caves Joan is luring you into."

"Now, Mr. Anders," Joan protested. "That wasn't a brilliant thing to say."

"So I'd suggest you wait a while, Anna," Jonathan said. "Sorry, Joan, we each have to paddle our own canoe."

"Truly, I find it difficult to decide which one of you is lying and which one telling the truth," Anna grumbled. "However, they cannot reach us for at least half an hour, even if we stand still. So we shall continue. But please hurry, Fräulein Benderer. And do please remember that if your soldier friends catch up with us, I shall be left with no alternative but to kill you. All of you."

"Sure and let's hurry then," Joan said, and set off across the hilltop, Pat at her elbow. "It's not far."

Jonathan threw a last look over his shoulder at the distant car. It was still a long way away, only visible because they had both been on the top of a hill. It had yet to descend into the valley and come across the ruins of Anna's rubber boulder. He hoped they managed to miss that. Much depended on how much Tim had had to drink.

Supposing they got past that, next stop the village, and Dorinda's car. That would give them something to think about. And even if they decided to ignore that, they'd soon come across the Rolls, parked at the foot of the path they had to take. But that would hardly put them off, he reckoned. If they meant to move the guns tonight, it could only be because they'd noticed that he and Pete had gone, presumably for assistance. The sight of the Rolls would only make them hurry the more.

"We go in here," Joan said. "We have to crawl for a while. Could we have our hands free?"

"Of course you may not," Anna said. "You can manage, I'm sure." She stooped, shone her light into the aperture. "It does not seem much like a cave to me. It just looks like a hole in the rock."

"That's why it's so difficult to find," Joan pointed out.

"I'm not going in there," Dorinda declared. "Oh, no. I've heard about these Kiltone caves. You'll have to carry me."

"Which is obviously impossible," Anna said. "Ah, well, Dorinda, I'm sorry it had to come to this. But of course you'll realize that we can't leave you here. Tigran, you may hit Miss Wantage on the head now. Do it rather hard, so she'll be sure to remain unconscious for some time."

"Don't you *dare*," Dorinda squealed. "Just don't. All right, Anna. All right. I'll come."

"Then I suggest we start crawling."

Jonathan watched her disappear behind Joan and Pat into the darkness. She still carried her pistol in her right hand, but she had slung her flashlight around her neck by its lanyard, and the bobbling light played over Pat's back. That was all the light she needed at this moment; so long as she could see Pat, Joan would not dare run away. He crawled into the entrance, felt the stone brush his back, and was pushed from behind by Vassily. He crawled as best he could, extending both hands as far forward as they would reach, and then bringing up his knees one by one behind them, but it was slow, painful work; the slope seemed much steeper now he was going downward, and he fell over several times. But he figured he wasn't the only one having trouble; the entire passageway behind him was filled with heavy breathing and uncontrolled slitherings.

"It's all right now," Joan whispered, the sound of her voice seeping backward through the gloom. "We can stand. But stay close if ye don't want to get lost; there are several passageways leading off this one."

They scrambled to their feet and followed the bobbing light. It was difficult to retain, to remember, a sense of direction, but it occurred to Jonathan that they were exactly retracing their steps of last night, when Joan had led them out. Why? The time was well after nine o'clock, so surely . . .

They debouched into a wider passage, which immediately led them into the arms cavern. Anna paused to shine her light over the boxes of rifles.

"Well, well, well," she said. "So you were telling the truth after all, Jonathan. Supposing these *are* intended for Northern Ireland, I would say your government had problems." She bent over one of the cases. "From Poland, I see. Oh, they are an enterprising lot, the Poles."

"Then you'll agree I was also right that that carload of nervous gunmen will be heading in this direction," Jonathan said.

"Oh, I do, indeed. You would not have had this in mind in bringing us here, Fräulein Benderer?"

"If ye want me father's notes, Miss Cantelna, this is the only way ye'll get them."

181

"Hmm," Anna said. "Thus it is necessary to hurry even more, I would say. How much farther do we have to go?"

"Not far," Joan said. "Down that passage over there."

"Very well, then, let us go on," Anna said.

Time to start listening for the tide, Jonathan decided. If only he knew what Joan had in mind.

The same thought had occurred to Tigran. He muttered something in Russian and pointed to the water mark on the cavern walls.

"Wait," Anna said, as Joan was about to disappear into the lower entrance. "The tide reaches up here?"

"Sure and of course it does," Joan said. "We're not more than twenty feet above the beach, down here. But only a few inches of water will get this far up," she pointed to her ankles, "and it won't be that high for another hour."

"But that passage slopes downward," Anna objected. "You expect me to believe that you concealed your father's papers beyond here? Below the high-water mark?"

"Sure and it's the truth," Joan said. "But if ye don't want them, after all . . ."

Anna hesitated. It was only the second time that Jonathan had ever seen her undecided. And it only lasted a couple of seconds.

"So we have two reasons for hurrying now," she said. "Go on, Fräulein."

They followed the sloping passageway downward, and now they could hear the noise of the breakers, whipped up by the rising wind, pounding on the beach.

"Are you certain it will not come in here for an hour?" Anna asked.

"Sure, I'm sure it won't *bother* us for an hour," Joan said. "It sounds much nearer than it is. The cave makes it sound closer."

They walked a few feet farther, and then Joan checked. "We turn off here," she said, and pointed with her chin at what was nothing more than a crack in the rock, barely wide enough for her to pass through, and not really practical for the three big Russian men. Jonathan didn't much care for its size, either.

"In there?" Anna demanded.

"That's where it is, Miss Cantelna."

"Hmm," Anna said. "Very well. You and I will get them. You four will line up against that wall. And Tigran, you and Vassily and Ewfim will face them. Do not take your pistols off them for a moment. And do not take the light off them for a moment, either. Is this a deep chasm, Fräulein Benderer?"

"Only a couple of feet," Joan said, and sidled into the opening. Anna followed, and they disappeared. No one in the outer passage spoke; they were all listening to various sounds. They heard footsteps scraping over the rock floor, just audible over the rumble of the surf, and then there was a whisper of sound from their own feet, and a ripple of icy water soaked their already sopping shoes.

"Ooooh!" Dorinda squealed. "What's that?"

"The sea," Jonathan told her.

The water had apparently also entered the chasm. "I hope you are right about the tide." Anna's voice came from surprisingly close. "And look, the passage ends there."

"Sure it does," Joan agreed. "I told ye it wasn't far. The papers are up there. See that ledge? That's above high-water level. But they're in an oilskin bag, anyway. I hid them there myself. Because I figured everyone would think just like ye, and even if they came looking, they'd stop at the high-water mark."

"You are a very smart child, after all," Anna said. "Now climb up there and get them. And please hurry."

"Sure and how can I do any climbing, Miss Cantelna, with my hands tied and all?"

"Then I will release your hands," Anna said. "Wait a moment." There were several seconds of silence, disturbed only by the lapping of the water and the noise of their own breathing. "There," Anna said at last. "Now climb away. And remember that my pistol is trained on you all the while."

There was a scrabbling sound as Joan went up.

"Have you got them?" Anna called.

"Sure, they're here."

"Well, then, come on. Hurry. This water is rising very quickly."

"You can say that again," Dorinda wailed. "It's up to my knees. We're going to drown. I just know we're going to drown."

"Sure and what d'ye think I'm doing?" Joan complained, "but hurrying."

"Now hurry back out," Anna commanded, and Joan emerged back into the passageway, flushed and panting, with grit and sand sticking to her wet hair. Anna followed, an oilskin package in her hands.

Tigran muttered something in Russian.

"Let me have a look at what we have got first, Tigran," Anna said. "I would not put it past this young lady to play another trick on us. Here, take my pistol. Vassily, hold the light over here." She knelt, up to her thighs in the surging water now, but seemingly quite undisturbed. Jonathan wondered if she had ever felt fear, or even alarm, at any moment in her life. Not fear, perhaps; but she could feel excitement. Her fingers were trembling as she untied the oiled cord fastening the package. Jonathan realized that she really was anxious to have Benderer's notes. Because it was good for the Soviet Union? Or because, beneath it all, she was an utterly dedicated scientist, and here in her hands, perhaps, was one of the most important scientific discoveries of all time. He rather hoped it was the second.

The package fell open, and inside it was a notebook with several sheets of foolscap wrapped around it. Anna unfolded the foolscap, and Vassily held the light closer. Anna glanced at the writing, nodded, carefully refolded them, looked instead at the notebook. She flipped over one or two pages, nodded again. "These are Otto's notes," she said. "I will need my laboratory before I can tell if they are of any value. But they are certainly his. Thank you, my child. Believe me, I am grateful, and I am truly sorry that there had to be so much unpleasantness about them." She stood up. "Now I think we should be out of here as rapidly as possible." She frowned. "What is that noise?"

"I rather think that Mick and the boys have arrived," Jonathan said.

The voices were quite distinct, booming down the corridor. Although they must have seen the cars, and would have to expect that Pete and Jonathan were somewhere either on the hillside or in the caves, they did not seem bothered. Or perhaps they hoped that a great deal of noise would lure their antagonists out of hiding.

"Let's get a move on now," Mick said. "Those two fellows will be back at any time, and I want these guns far away by then."

"And sure if we don't, we'll be after getting wet feet," Paddy said.

"Switch off those lights," Anna whispered, and the lower passageway was plunged into darkness. "Is there another way out of here?"

"Only by the beach," Joan said. "Sure and it's too late for that now."

"You had better hope not," Anna said. "Go first." She switched on her own flashlight again, directing it away from the munitions cave. "Hurry, now."

Joan hesitated, and then shrugged and led them down the passage. They resumed their original order, and Tigran also switched on his light again. But now the water was deepening very quickly. By the time they reached the entrance to the first cave it was up to their chests, and poor Pat was in it to her neck.

"Oh, we can't go any farther," Dorinda wailed. "We'll be drowned."

"Keep your voice down," Anna hissed.

"But she's right," Joan said. "Look, the entrance is submerged. It's just a hole in the rock, ye know, Miss Cantelna. That means there's five feet of water out there on the beach."

"And big waves, too," Jonathan said. "Judging by the movement in here."

"Ye're stuck," Pat said.

Anna's expression never changed; her face, only just visible in the glow from the lamp, was as resolutely firm as Jonathan could ever remember, and as calmly confident. "I have no doubt at all that you planned just this ending to our little expedition, Fräulein Benderer," she said. "And I congratulate you. I think where you may have made your mistake was in your judgment of the people involved. As I remember, there were only five young men at the dance, and as we only saw one car coming over the hill, there can hardly be more than five young men in that cave up there. There are four of us, we are armed, probably better than our opponents, even if they may be surrounded by weapons, and we shall also have the advantage of surprise. So then"—she looked at her three aides—"we shall shoot our way out."

CHAPTER 8

"Sure and if ye do that ye'll have the roof in," Joan objected.

Anna turned to Tigran, who hesitated, and then nodded.

"Hmm," she said. "Well, then, we shall have to wait for your friends to finish their task. It should not take so very long. You will lead us back up to where our heads at least will remain above water, Fräulein Benderer."

"Pat's head, ye mean," Joan said. "That'll be quite a way. Come on."

"Oh, Lord," Dorinda said. "Oh, Lord. I'm freezing. And I'm sure there are fish in here. Do fish ever come in here, Joan?"

"Not if they can help it, Miss Wantage," Joan said. "Ye might get the odd eel, now and then."

"Eels?" Dorinda squealed. "Oh, Lord. I'm going to faint."

"I wish you would," Anna snapped. "And please be quiet about it."

They made their way back up the passage, a succession of faint splashes, lost at any distance, Jonathan estimated, by the crashing of the waves against the outer cavern; each roller seemed to shake the entire cliff. It was a rugged night out there. And what sort of a night was it going to be in here? If Anna waited until Mick and the boys had cleared the rifles, there'd be nothing to stop her shooting the five of them and leaving them down here. Would she do that? Would she have any real alternative? She couldn't afford to have them following her, especially as she still had several hours on Irish soil before she could catch a flight back to Leningrad. And Anna was not the sort of person to let *any*thing stand in the way of completing a mission. In which case . . .

He bumped into her. Joan had checked, just beyond the entrance to the chasm in which she had hidden her father's papers. Here they were still waist deep in the icy water, which came surging past them in a succession of ripples. But now they could see the glow of the light from in front of them, and they could hear the tramping of feet.

"We will stay here," Anna whispered, and switched off her flashlight. Tigran promptly also doused his. "And not a sound," Anna whispered. "From anyone."

"One more load will do it," Mick panted, his voice echoing down the corridor. "And ye know what, lads? In the circumstances, and seeing that we're in a hurry, we'll borrow the old nutter's Rolls to take a couple of the cases. Ye'll like that, George, eh, driving a Rolls?"

"That's stealing," Joe objected.

"Borrowing," Mick pointed out. "Sure and we'll have it to Sligo and back long before dawn."

"I wonder what it's doing there," Tim said. "Them fellows must be somewhere around."

"I told ye," Mick said. "It's not them fellows at all. It's the Russian bit, looking for old George's secrets. Supposing he had any. Well, if she's down here without Joan, she's welcome to stay."

"And what about the sports job?" Paddy demanded. "And Joan and me crazy sister? They took me cart. Did ye know that, Mick? They took me cart."

"Sure and I don't understand that at all," Mick said. "But ye'll have to admit that the English chap isn't here. Maybe he was telling the truth after all, and he is after the madam. Sure and why not? I really don't see how he can have known about the guns. Anyway, our job is to move this stuff, so just get a move on."

"Ooooh!" Dorinda screamed, the sound welling upward through the cavern.

There was a crash from in front of them. "Cripes, and what's that?" Joe demanded.

"Sounded like a banshee, it did," Paddy complained.

"Something touched me!" Dorinda howled. "Something touched me! Something cold! It's an eel! Oooh!"

"Will you be quiet," Anna snapped.

"Help!" Dorinda screamed. "Mick, help me. It's Dorinda Wantage!"

"Tigran," Anna said.

There was a tremendous splash as Tigran swung his pistol.

But apparently he had missed. "Ooooh!" Dorinda screamed. "He tried to hit me. Mick! Help me, Mick!"

The lights in front of them had gone out, and now there was silence as well.

"Who's down there?" Mick called. "Miss Wantage, is that really ye?"

"It's me as well, Mick," Joan called. "And Pat. We're being held by the Russians."

"Damn you, child," Anna said, and fired.

It was not a terribly loud explosion, but it reverberated through the caverns and was followed by a whole series of splashes. Jonathan lunged forward and grappled someone; he supposed it was Anna, because it was a woman and she turned round and struck at him, although she never said a word.

"Pat!" Paddy was shouting. "Pat, are ye in there? Pat? Is that ye?"

"Here I am," Pat gasped, bursting into the arms cavern. She had taken the opportunity to duck under the surface and escape. "My wrists are tied."

Jonathan's hands slipped on the body he was holding, and his head went under the water as he sank to the floor of the corridor. Someone kicked him. He got back to his feet, against the farther wall, and heard a whole series of explosions, some from close at hand—no doubt as Tigran and his two companions got into the act—and another even louder, from up front as Paddy fired his shotgun. Bullets crunched into the stone, but apparently, and amazingly, no one was hit, although there was so much noise it was difficult to tell for certain. Jonathan flattened himself against the wall, trying to identify shapes in the darkness, listening to enough splashes to suggest there was an entire shoal of fish in here, the whole punctuated by shouts from the boys in the upper cave and a continuous high-pitched screaming sound from Dorinda.

"Mick!" Joan called from in front of Jonathan. "Mick! Don't shoot. It's me, Joan. Mr. Rodgers? Mr. Rodgers? Pete? Where are ye, Pete?"

"I'm not sure," Pete replied, also from the front of the corridor, Jonathan realized to his surprise; he must have taken advantage of the confusion to get away from Vassily.

"This way," Joan said. "This way. We're coming out, Mick."

There was another tremendous explosion as one of the Russians fired. The noise echoed round and round the narrow corridor and was succeeded by a sinister creaking noise.

"Joan?" Mick asked. "Is that ye, Joan? Well, then, we're all here. Except for Miss Wantage."

"Don't leave me!" Dorinda screamed. She was still at the back. "Don't leave me in here!"

"And Mr. Anders," Pat said. "I don't know where he has got to at all."

"Tigran," Anne whispered. Her voice came from beside him, Jonathan realized. "Tigran, where are you?"

"I am here," Tigran said in Russian. He was standing on Jonathan's other side.

"And where *is* Mr. Anders?" Anna asked.

"I do not know, Madame Cantelna."

"He tried to grapple with me," Anna said. "And I threw him off. I think he may have been hit by one of those bullets." She sighed. "What a stupid, wasteful world this is, Tigran. But listen. I think the girl may have been right when she said shooting would cause some of this rock to fall. We must get out, and quickly. We will rush the cave. If they switch on their lights, we will shoot them out. You understand me? But we must keep going."

"No," Tigran said. "*We* will rush them, Madame Cantelna. You stay here. You have the papers. We will draw their fire, and them as well, and then you can leave."

"I cannot permit you to do that for me, Tigran," Anna said. "At the very least, if you fail to break through, you will be sent to prison."

"In which case you will apply for our deportation back to the Soviet Union," Tigran pointed out. "There is no time for argument, Madame. My orders were to get you into this country, and even more important, get you back out, unharmed, and if possible with these papers. But you are more important than even the papers. I cannot risk your being hurt. Now wait here until we have cleared a way for you."

Jonathan pressed himself flat against the wall as Tigran waded past him, followed by the other two. He figured the tide was still rising; it had reached his chest. If only his hands were free. But at least he'd have the advantage of surprise.

"You can't leave me!" Dorinda screamed. "Not here. Wait a moment. Something's happening!"

"Switch on your light," Mick commanded. "Shine it on the entrance. Now, Paddy, is your gun loaded?"

"It's loaded," Paddy promised.

"But say, what about Jon?" Pete demanded. "He's still in there."

"I'm very much afraid that Mr. Anders is dead," Anna called. "Believe me, Mr. Rodgers, I grieve for him just as much as you do. Now surely it would be senseless to have any more killing. Why do you not withdraw from that cave to the surface, and we will come out. Tell your Irish friends that we are not interested in their weapons. We only wish to leave."

"Don't believe her," Pat said. "Oh, she's a devil, that one."

"And she has me dad's papers," Joan protested. "We can't let her get away with them."

"Ye're trapped, Miss Cantelna," Mick called. The light was on now, glowing in the entrance to the arms cave, but not penetrating the corridor, where, if anything, the distant gleam made the darkness more intense. "Throw out your weapons and we'll not harm ye."

"Wait for me!" Dorinda called. "I'm coming out. Aaagh! I touched something. Something cold and wet and horrible. Aaagh!"

Jonathan threw her hands away from him, shrank back into the darkness. Anna was still within a few feet of him. And Anna would soon be alone. She would suppose she was alone, with Otto Benderer's papers somewhere on her person.

Dorinda was still screaming, and wading up the passageway. "Aaagh!" she screamed again. "Someone's holding me."

"Now!" Tigran bellowed in Russian. He had obviously seized her as a shield. "Now!"

194

"Don't shoot!" Dorinda screamed. "He's got me. Don't shoot!"

But Paddy fired, nonetheless, although it must have been at the roof, Jonathan reasoned, because there were no cries of pain and at that range he could hardly have missed.

It *had* been at the roof. There was a sudden rumble from above them which steadily grew in intensity, and a lump of rock brushed Jonathan's face before splashing into the water. In front of him the noise was at its loudest, and the cave was filled with splashings.

"Aaagh!" Dorinda screamed again. "Aaagh!"

"It's coming in," Mick was yelling. "Get out, lads. Get out. And be sure ye have the girls."

"Jon!" Pete shouted. "Are you in there, Jon? For pity's sake, we can't just leave him."

"Ye'll be dead too, sure, Mr. Rodgers, if ye go back in there," Tim said.

"Come on, ye great Commie lummox," Mick shouted. "That gun's no use to ye now."

Tigran was shouting in Russian, but obviously all three of them were also on the other side of the fall, because now the whole cliff was trembling, and endless rock was plummeting down into the turbulent water, and not so far away either. Jonathan reached into the darkness, got his hands on Anna's shoulders and pulled her backward.

She gave a little gasp. "Who's that?" she asked.

"Your friend and mine," Jonathan promised her.

"Jonathan!" She sounded genuinely relieved. "So you weren't hit after all. Oh, you are a crafty boy." She switched on the flashlight she still held in her left hand, played it over him for a moment, and then stood on tiptoe to kiss him on the cheek. "I'm glad. There are too few people in this world who are at once talented and nice to know." The light swung away from him, illuminated the corridor behind them. Now there was nothing visible at all, except a huge mass of rock which had fallen from the ceiling and blocked the entire passage; the air was filled with dust. The noises still rumbled around them, but seemed to be decreasing. "To think that we were standing there only a few minutes ago," she said. "I hope they all got out."

"So do I," Jonathan agreed. "Anna, in the circumstances in which we now find ourselves, do you think you'd like to untie my hands?"

She smiled at him. "No, I do not think that would be a terribly good idea, Jonathan. They do not really hinder your movements in any way." She frowned. "Listen."

"Halloooo!" Mick shouted, his voice seeming to come from very far away. "Is anybody there?"

"Yes," Anna called. "We are here. Jonathan is with me. He is all right after all."

"Well, listen," Mick shouted. "There's been a big fall. The rock is too big to move. But in another four hours the tide will have gone back far enough for ye to get out and onto the beach. We'll look for ye there."

"That is very kind of you," Anna said.

"Sure and it's no trouble," Mick said. "D'ye have a light at all?"

"Oh, yes, we have a light," Anna said. "If the

water were not so cold we would be quite comfortable. How are my three compatriots?"

"They're here, Miss Cantelna," Mick said. "Unharmed. And unarmed, now, too. So ye'll see your little game is up."

"Are you there, Jon?" Pete shouted.

"I'm here," Jonathan said. "See you in a couple of hours."

"So keep smiling," Pete said.

Anna smiled. "They are so thoughtful. And at least we are not buried alive. I should not like to be buried alive. Which is why I never doubted that to threaten her friend with such a fate would very rapidly persuade Miss Herries to tell me what I wanted to know. Believe me, I did not wish to do it."

"I'm sure you didn't," Jonathan agreed. "Well, we may not be quite buried, but has it occurred to you that we're well and truly stuck in? When we come out onto that beach, we're both prisoners. Sure, Pete may talk them into believing that I'm only interested in you, and sure they may just stick you on the first plane back to Russia, but they'll relieve you of that paper first."

The light, which had been playing over the rockfall, came back to his face. From the glow he was able to see her frown. "I had not thought of that. Perhaps we should try to get out now. I seem to remember that you are a good underwater swimmer. So am I. How far would we have to go?"

"Too far, especially as that light doesn't look too waterproof to me. Anyway, that's surf out there. Big waves. We'd be knocked apart in seconds."

"I suppose you are right," she said thoughtfully. "But I still think we should try to get out. Let's see if there are any more side passages leading upward." She brushed past him, paused to glance at him. "Aren't you coming?"

"If you'll untie my wrists."

She put her head on one side. "A truce, then. An alliance. Until we are rid of these overenthusiastic gun runners."

"Done. You still have your little pistol, haven't you?"

"It is a great comfort to me." She thrust the gun beneath the surface, into her pocket, and took out a small knife instead, with which she slit the rope securing his wrists. "And if you do happen to get any wild ideas, Jonathan, I must assure you that the water will not affect the pistol in the least. Now come."

She led him back down the corridor, but there were no openings save Joan's chasm, and every second they sank deeper into the sea. Anna persisted until the water was lapping at her mouth, and she was carrying the light above her head. "It is not possible," she said.

"What about Joan's little hideaway?"

"It really *is* little. Barely twelve feet deep."

"But Joan climbed up, so there must be a fault in the rock. There could be an opening higher up."

"You are full of ideas, Jonathan. How I wish we were working together, you and I." She retraced her steps, Jonathan at her elbow.

"We are working together, Anna. To get out of here. Remember?"

"Oh, yes. I had forgotten. Here we are." She

inserted herself into the opening. "Can you get through? It is much broader inside."

Jonathan forced himself through the narrow crevasse, leaving behind him a couple of buttons and even a strip of skin, but otherwise unharmed. "Shine the light upward," he said.

Anna obeyed, but after about twenty feet the beam dwindled into the darkness. She allowed it to play over the rock face; it was pitted with holes, serrated with cuts and slight ledges. Climbing was not going to be difficult.

"What do you say?" he asked. "Worth a try?"

"Anything is worth a try," she agreed. "And it will get us out of this beastly cold water. Will you go first?"

"Okay. You shine the flash up to give me some light."

She nodded, and he swung himself up to the first handhold, hung there for a moment while water dripped from his clothes into the sea beneath. Onto Anna, as well.

"That is much colder," she said.

"I figure I'm shedding a couple of pounds of the stuff," he said. "It'll make climbing easier."

He started to go up, slowly and methodically, finding safe places for his hands and remembering their locations for his feet. It was at least warming, and by the time he had reached the limit of the light he was sweating. He looked down at the glow; he couldn't see Anna herself.

"Coming up?" His voice echoed.

"You will lose the light until I reach you," she said. "Just for a minute or two."

She hung it round her neck. He waited, listened to the soft scrabbling of her fingers, the scraping of her boots. Those sounds apart, the cliff was filled with the continuous rumble of the surf pounding on the rock, how far away, he wondered. But already the rocks to which he hung were dry. Although there was no sign of any opening, as yet.

Her hand touched his shoe, and she checked. "I am tired," she panted. "It has been a busy night. And yet a profitable one. Had you not interfered, and thereby caused that girl to come behind you, I would not have got Otto's papers."

"*We* would not have got Otto's papers," Jonathan reminded her.

"Of course I meant we," she said. "Do you see a traverse passage?"

"Shine the light upward."

The beam played on him and then past him. The crevasse, or perhaps, more accurately a funnel disappeared into the cliff.

"Nothing on the sides," he said. "Yet, anyway. Say, there's a thought. Maybe it goes straight out into the hilltop."

"You are an optimist," she said. "It is blowing half a gale outside. If this were open to the sky, there would be a tremendous volume of air funneling down. But there is no movement of air at all."

"And you," he pointed out, "are too much of a realist. So here goes."

Climbing was easier now, because the funnel was distinctly narrower, and it was possible to lean back from time to time and rest his back against the opposite wall. By the same token he figured they might soon run out of space altogether. And suddenly he did jar himself on a piece of rock projecting from behind him, which bit into his shoulder and made him lose one of his handholds and slip down a few feet.

"Are you all right?" Anna called.

"Just. You want to watch it when you're coming up."

"It is getting narrower, eh? Is there any use in going on?"

"Well, I'm not sure." He twisted round as far as he could, wedged now against the spur which had halted him. Beyond, the funnel was again wider, and he couldn't see the opposite wall. But it looked very dark. "I'll need the flash."

"Wait there." He looked down again, watched her come up, the flash in her hand, making her way toward him. Her face, normally so perfectly made up, perfectly relaxed, was drawn with effort and fatigue and covered with several layers of dust, clinging to the still wet skin and coating the normally jet black hair, which was itself wisping rather than clinging to her scalp. She had discarded her raincoat, and her velvet pants suit was torn at both knees, as well as being also coated with dust and grit. Anything less like the typical Anna Cantelna could hardly be imagined. But as she came closer he saw that her eyes had not changed; they were as magnetically alive and intensely thoughtful as ever he remembered them. It occurred to him that Anna's eyes would not change until the moment she died.

She smiled at him, still panting faintly, as she came up to just below him. "What is your problem?"

"Over there. Just beyond the spur."

She directed the beam of light. The opposite wall of the funnel was now perhaps six feet away, and the flashlight beam, moving slowly from left to right, was swallowed by a more intense blackness, perhaps four feet across and about the same in height.

Anna's breath came sharply. "You think that is an opening?"

"I don't see what else it can be."

"But you will have to jump. If it is not . . ."

"You'll be on your own. In which case I suggest you admit defeat and go back down to wait for our friends."

The light came back, settled on his face. "I do not know if I should let you. Courage is one thing, but . . ."

"I'm not really taking a risk, believe me. I don't believe in them. That has to be an opening."

"Wait a moment." She forced herself higher, until she was almost on his level, but still the light only lost itself in the darkness opposite them. "It is at least six feet away," she said. "And no space to take a run at it."

"So I'll go above it. Hold the light steady." He climbed past her, looked down on the passage entrance—if it *was* a passage entrance. But certainly they couldn't climb much farther; the funnel narrowed once again immediately above his head.

"Okay," he said. "Keep that flash fixed on the wall over there, Anna. So here goes nothing."

He sucked air into his lungs until he thought they would burst, at the same time tensed every muscle, worked his fingers to make sure they were supple, pressed his back into the rock behind him, and then propelled himself into space. For what seemed an interminable moment he was falling, and then he struck the opposite wall with a jar which knocked all the breath from his body. Desperately he threw his arms forward, felt them slipping on smooth rock for an agonizing second, and then his left hand lodged on an outcrop, perhaps three feet in. There was at least a ledge.

"Jonathan?" Anna's voice was sharp. "Are you all right?"

His entire weight still hung from his left hand. He swept his right over the rock in front of him, while his fingers commenced to burn and he could feel the stone beginning to cut his flesh. He decided he could wait no longer, drove his right elbow down on to the rock and forced himself upward before it could slip, threw his left leg over the ledge, hung again for a moment while he struggled for breath, and then heaved himself over, rolling into space. There was no wall. It was, indeed, an opening, stretching into the rock, disappearing blackly behind him.

"Jonathan!" Anna shouted. "Are you all right?"

He crawled back to the ledge, still panting, every muscle shuddering with the effort. "I think so. There is an opening into some sort of a passageway. I have no idea where it leads. Are you coming?"

"I suppose so." She sounded doubtful. But that was the thought of the jump, surely; there was no risk of her backing out at this stage, he figured. She would regard him as less of a threat to her possession of Otto Benderer's papers than Mick and the boys, especially when supported by Pete.

"Toss me the light, then."

She lobbed the flashlight toward him. He caught it in both hands, laid it on the ledge beside him, wedged against the corner of the passage, so that it shone into the void, illuminating the lip toward which she must come, and the rock wall facing it.

"Now," he instructed. "Climb a bit higher, as I did, and then throw yourself forward. And it must be a good jump, Anna; no doubts. I'll catch you."

She gazed into the light beam for a moment; she could not see his face behind the glare. Her tongue, small and pink, came out and circled her lips. It occured to him that Anna Cantelna was frightened. No, that wasn't true. Anna was apprehensive, weighing her chances of survival, summoning all her mental powers to come to her aid. Then she turned her face toward the rock wall again and went up, hand over hand.

"That's far enough," he said. "If you turn now, you'll find you can wedge your feet fairly well, so you will be able to give yourself a good send-off."

She turned slowly. "You will catch me, Jonathan?"

"I said I would, Anna."

He watched her sucking air into her lungs. He wondered what was passing through her mind at that moment. He had thought of nothing but the ledge opposite. To think of the water at the bottom of the funnel, of the projecting rocks she would strike on the way down, would be a dreadful mistake.

She came forward with agonizing slowness, legs spreading as she left the rock, arms cartwheeling, for she had pushed off with her palms as well. He fought against the temptation to rise to his knees and lean out over the chasm; he would require all of his weight anchored to the rock on which he lay to prevent them both from plummeting downward, but he realized to his horror that she was not coming as fast as he had done.

She struck the rock, a glancing blow, and at the same moment screamed, "Jonathan!"

She was already slipping down the smooth face, fingers scrabbling helplessly at the rock. Jonathan caught her left wrist. For the most terrible moment he could ever remember her flesh slipped through his grasp, and then he closed both his hands on hers.

"Help me," she begged, her voice a thin whisper of sound.

Jonathan reached for breath. "Easy, now," he said. "Easy." He wriggled backward into the darkness. Her left hand came over the ledge, drawn by his weight, and now she swung her right hand over it. He watched her fingers searching the ledge, without success, spread his own legs so that each foot was anchored to a wall of the passage. "Over me," he gasped. "Climb over me."

The fingers of her right hand ate into his arm, and then his shoulder. For a moment she held his hair, and he groaned with pain. Then she was on to his jacket, and the fingers of her left hand moved against his. He released her, and she swung that arm in turn, bringing the hand down to grip his sleeve. Now her entire weight rested on his clothes, and he felt himself beginning to slip forward.

"Hurry," he begged.

Anna gasped, and threw herself upward and forward. Jonathan's mouth bit the lip of the ledge itself, and he stared down into space, but she was clear now, above him and on the rock floor beside him. Her legs still flailed as they came up. One boot struck him behind the ear and sent a shaft of pain through his already aching head. The other flicked the flashlight neatly out of its wedge in the rock. For a moment the glow circled through the air, and then it struck on the rocks immediately beneath them and went out.

They listened to the clattering, growing distant until it ended with a faint splash. Then there was almost silence. The darkness was Stygian, and frighteningly still. Up here, the surf seemed very far away, and the cavern was filled only with the gasping of their own breathing.

"I will never do anything like that again," Anna said. "I will never be able to make myself. I am sorry about the light, Jonathan."

"Can't be helped. Better the light than you." He felt her move from his back, pushed himself up to his hands and knees, wiped sweat from his brow.

"But what will we do now?" she asked.

"Follow our noses, I think. This must go somewhere. What we really have to worry about is side passages leading off. So I'll tell you what we'll do. I'll stick to this side and you stick to yours, and we'll touch each other every other step, just to make sure we're both still here."

"Yes," she agreed. "That would be a very good idea. You think of everything, Jonathan."

They crawled, Jonathan on the left of the passage, Anna just behind him on the right. Every five seconds he stretched out his right hand and found her left, cold and already dry. He also tried the roof, but it remained too low for standing. They listened to their breathing, to the rustle of their movements. Now they could hardly hear the surf at all.

"I have to rest," Anna gasped after about half an hour. "This has been the most exhausting day of my life. When I think of the amount of energy I wasted this morning on that stupid, wasteful hunt. Why are men such fools, Jonathan?"

"Answer that one and we wouldn't have any more problems," he said, and sat beside her. "The world, I mean."

"You have no idea how helpless I sometimes feel," she complained. "As now, indeed. I am a genius. Present me with a mathematical problem, ask me something, anything, about marine life, even require of me a detailed and accurate political judgment, and I will be able to answer you in seconds. So here I find myself, crawling about the middle of some ancient mountain, unable to find my way out. Do you think there is a way out, Jonathan?"

"I think there is."

"Why? Why should there be? What about the tale your little Irish friend was telling us about the smuggler who was trapped in here and wandered forever?"

"A legend. Although I suppose it's possible. But I'll tell you one thing for sure, he died of hunger and thirst, not suffocation."

"Oh, yes," she said. "I know what you are thinking. There is still enough air. So there must be an opening to the sky, somewhere. But there is no guarantee that we will find it without a light."

"We'll find it," he promised her. "Have you had any side turnings?"

"No," she admitted.

"So let's go. Come on. It can't be far."

They crawled, staring ahead of them into the blackness, waiting for a glimpse of the lighter darkness of the night. Jonathan felt they were slowly describing a circle—why, he could not be sure; he was not even sure which way they were turning. But if they were, of course, there was a chance that they were doubling back. That would be a blow, if the passage came out halfway up or down the cliff face. Although as he and Pete had managed to climb down ... could it be only last night? He wondered if Anna would be able to manage a climb. He thought her nerves were getting just a little bit ragged. Was that at all surprising? Not in any woman save Anna.

A cloud of stinging, swinging branches swept into his face, forced him to stop with an exclamation of pain mingled with alarm.

"Jonathan!" Anna snapped from just behind him. "Jonathan! What has happened?"

"Just some kind of a plant, growing up in the ..." He parted the branches. "Hold on. Glory be. It's a bush growing out of the tunnel mouth." He stood up in the fresh air and the dripping rain and inhaled. Nothing had ever felt quite so good.

"Jonathan!" Anna stood beside him, gripped his arm. "You know, I was beginning to doubt? But where are we?"

He was trying to decide. On the slope away from the cliff, certainly, because it was a gentle incline and there was no sea in sight, although once again they could hear the surf.

"We want to go to the right," he said. "Come on."

They ran across the soft grass, tired as they were. Perhaps he had been beginning to doubt, too. Certainly he had no wish to enter that network of caves again. Or any network of caves, for that matter. And now he was out, he was realizing how tired he was, too. How sleepy, how physically exhausted. But now was the last time to relax.

"Look," Anna said. "The Rolls."

They had been descending as they ran, and now they had arrived on the landward side of the cemetery. The graves glistened in the rain, and beyond, on the path, the huge car waited patiently.

"And Tim's taxi." It was parked just behind the Rolls. "I wonder where our friends have got to." He looked at his watch. "For Pete's sake, do you know we were in that beastly place for three hours? It's all but one."

"Then they will have gone down to the beach to look for us," she said. "We must hurry."

She began to run again, splashing through the mud. "Do not worry," she said. "The keys are in the car."

"And what then?"

She glanced at him, almost is if she had forgotten why they were there.

"We could go back to the castle and photograph Otto's stuff," he said. "As we agreed. And then both be on our ways."

Anna said nothing, continued to jog at his side, panting.

"But of course, you'll want to get your three pals out of hock," he said thoughtfully.

"There is always something." Anna slowed to a walk as they approached the car. "Oh, my, I seem to have been running, and crawling, and straining all day. I don't think I shall ever be the same. I shall become like Dorinda Wantage, and spend my time complaining that my clothes are ruined. As indeed they are."

"I'll drive," Jonathan decided.

"No," she said, and she had allowed herself again to drop behind him.

He turned, gazed at the little pistol. "Do you know, I really felt that this time we'd manage to stay on the same wavelength? Anyway, I never thought you'd go back on your word."

"We are out of the cave now, Jonathan."

"The word was free of our trigger-happy gun runners, as I remember. You won't be free of them until you're clear of Kiltone, Anna."

"I disagree with you. Whatever I said, I *meant* out of the cave. Now, as I really do not wish to shoot you, will you please lie down. On your back, if you will, so that you will have difficulty in rising quickly. It need not be for very long."

She had retreated while she was speaking. He could reach her in a single bound. It all depended on whether or not she would really shoot.

She seemed able to read his thoughts, as usual. "Oh, yes," she said. "I will shoot you if you try to attack me. Believe me, Jonathan. I value you, and your friendship, very highly indeed. But I value my country, my duty, my responsibility, more."

Jonathan sighed and sat down, and then lay down. The ground was cold, but surprisingly firm, at this point, as Anna had also noticed; she stamped twice, then backed away from him, opened the taxi door, glanced inside. "Good. They have taken their keys. They are thoughtful young men." She moved along to the Rolls, sat behind the wheel, but left the door open and the pistol pointed at him while she started the engine. "Believe me, Jonathan, I am, and I forever will be, grateful to you for saving my life back in that horrible cavern. I hope we will meet again, in happier circumstances. Until then." The door slammed, the car moved forward, but was already turning to the left, off the path. She was going to reverse it round here, where the ground was hard, rather than try backing right along the path, with soft ground on either side and Tim's taxi in the way. It occurred to Jonathan that perhaps driving was one of the few skills Anna had never spared the time to master. In which case there was still a chance.

He rolled to one side, rose to his knees, watched the car swinging back toward him. He had never tried this one before. But she had to stop, for just a moment.

The Rolls checked as Anna braked and shifted from reverse to drive. Jonathan threw himself forward, got his feet on the bumper, his hands onto the handle for the trunk. The car moved forward again, and then slowed. She had felt the impact of his arrival. Then the car gathered speed again. She had decided not to risk stopping now. But she would be thinking, planning. What?

The Rolls roared into the village, slowed slightly as it struck the cobbles, then Anna gave it the gun again; the houses surged past before, without any warning, she braked. The car screamed to a halt, skidding sideways across the slippery stones and crashing into one of the white painted garden walls which bordered the road. Jonathan's hands slipped from the catch, and one foot went down to steady himself. Desperately he reached back to regain his hold, but already Anna was gunning the engines, and his fingers slipped. A cloud of exhaust fumes came up into his face and had him choking as he hit the ground.

For some seconds he was too dazed to move. Then he scrambled to his feet, and watched the rear lights of the Rolls disappearing into the first dip after the village. In the same instant he saw the dull gleam of Dorinda's sports car waiting by the far side of the street, almost invisible in the shade of the houses.

He staggered toward it, wiping blood from his chin where it had hit the cobbles and gashed. A distant shout made him glance over his shoulder; of course Mick would have left someone to watch the cars. Which made haste even more imperative. He threw open the door, got behind the wheel, turned the key. The engine started first kick, and gave a little roar of suppressed power. He turned the car and drove out of the village. Anna was not in sight, and the Rolls had twice as much horse power. But she had no reason to suppose she was being followed; he switched off his lights, steered by the bushes growing at the side of the road. The Rolls was also an automatic; if he could get close enough he might surprise her yet.

He put his foot flat on the floor, and the sports car tried to take off at the next hill. It settled with a crash, rocking to and fro, and he reminded himself to take it easy; he couldn't afford to have a blowout now. But the Rolls was back in his sight, traveling slowly; obviously Anna was looking for the remains of the rubber. And finding it. The car swung to the left, and then straightened again and gathered speed; Jonathan strained his eyes, saw the mass of crumpled rubber, followed Anna's example. As he brought the little car straight again, he instinctively glanced in his rear-view mirror and saw lights behind him. Tim! Or somebody in Tim's car. But he was using his headlights, the idiot, and was illuminating the whole road.

As he had feared, the lights caught Anna's attention, and he decided she must have seen him as well. The Rolls really began to travel, drawing away from him for a second or two before he regained his own maximum speed. Then he was gaining. Anna was driving as fast as she dared on the slippery surface, and indeed holding the little car straight was an effort requiring constant adjustment; the Rolls was several times as large, and if it ever got into a skid there'd be no stopping it. As Anna would learn.

Kiltone Castle loomed on their right, still a blaze of light, and no doubt merriment, despite the absence of all the young people of the village. He wondered if Anna would stop and try using Lord Wantage as a shield. But she had already decided against it, never even slowed at the gates, went roaring up the road toward Sligo. Of course, with typical Russian thoroughness, she would have been given a town address where she'd be able to get a change of clothes and no doubt an air ticket and transport to Shannon as well. But Joan Herries had said it was five miles to the nearest village. Five miles in which to take her. The longest of last laps.

Now the road straightened, and the Rolls' headlight beams seemed to stretch forever. And now she was only thirty yards in front. The big car was moving from side to side constantly. Because she was watching him in her mirror? Or as part of a definite plan to stop him drawing alongside? He suspected it might be a bit of both.

Now he switched on his own headlights, flicking them up to bright; Anna would have a tinted rear window, but the lights wouldn't do her morale any good. The movement of the Rolls became more violent; he was going to take a knock when he moved up. But so long as he got out fast enough he should be able to avoid being rolled over.

He was slipstreaming now, riding in the vacuum caused by the big car, gaining precious yards of speed, his lights glaring off the shining black crumpled rear wing where she had struck the wall. And ahead of them was a dog-leg bend in the road, together with a downward dip. Jonathan did a hasty calculation. Figuring, like Thorssen, she would slow down and drift to the outside of the road, he put his foot flat on the floor and turned in. Anna had already slackened speed, now threw a terrified glance over her shoulder as the searing headlights moved past. The sports car was already filling half the road. Anna tried to swing back, and for a heartcracking second the two cars touched. The night filled with the screaming of tortured metal, and Jonathan felt the sports car begin to move sideways. Then the pressure was gone. Anna's nerve had failed, and she had swung away again. But far too violently. For several moments Jonathan could not spare the time to look at her as he fought to control his own vehicle; then he realized she was no longer on the road.

He shifted down and braked, pulled open the car door and got out. The Rolls careered down the shallow slope beside the road, Anna twisting the wheel to and fro to maintain some semblance of control. Then it stopped with a suddenness which threw her forward against the windshield. Her head bobbed, and she disappeared.

Jonathan ran forward. The other car would be here at any moment, and he must secure the papers and be away. He was within six feet of the Rolls when something tugged at his ankle.

He checked and looked down, and then stared at the car again. It was already down to the hubcaps in just fifteen seconds; his own shoes were gripped by a terrifying force, sucking him downward. As Pete had said, you want to watch these Irish bogs.

He glanced over his shoulder. He could regain firm ground in a single bound, he figured. Then he gazed at the car again. It was beginning to sink. And Anna was still in the front seat, not moving, apparently knocked unconscious by the crack on her head.

He sucked air into his lungs, tensed his muscles,

and threw himself forward. The ground plucked off his shoes and he fell full length, but his hands closed on the rear bumper. Painfully he pulled himself forward, dragged himself clear of the oozing black mud, stood on the bumper itself; but his weight forced the rear of the car down and the bumper itself was half immersed.

Desperately he scrambled up the roof, slid across to the driver's side. There was just space for the door to swing. He hung upside down, thanked Heaven that Anna had been driving with the window open, pushed his hand in and released the catch. An effort forced the door open; Anna fell against it. He caught her by the hair just in time to prevent her from falling head first into the bog. Now he got his feet down, anchored them on the window, tucked his hands into her armpits and pulled her up. A moment later she was stretched beside him on the car roof, while he panted for breath and watched the door in utter horror. Once again his weight had tilted the car, and the door had dipped into the bog; it was a third gone.

Still hanging onto Anna with one hand, he dragged himself up the other side to even the slope. But they had to think about getting off; if that were still possible.

"Anna!" he shouted, shaking her shoulder. "Anna! Wake up."

Her eyes opened, and she frowned at him. "You forced me off the road," she muttered. "You were too determined for me yet again, Jonathan."

"Too determined for both of us," he pointed out.

She sat up, hastily clutched the roof. "But what has happened?"

"You drove into a sand trap, that's what happened. Now listen. Firm ground is over there. See. Any ideas on how we get there?"

"That is at least twelve feet," she said. "Can you jump twelve feet? I cannot."

"I might just," he said. "But not from a standing start."

"So we must think of something else. But there is that other car."

Tim's taxi pulled to a halt at the side of the road and unloaded Tim himself, Mick, Paddy O'Rourke, Joan and Pat, Dorinda Wantage, and last, and most welcome of all, Pete Rodgers. It must have been a tight fit, Jonathan decided.

"Well, glory be, Mr. Anders," Mick remarked. "Now there's a fine mess ye've got yourself into. D'ye know what they say around these parts? That bog has no bottom at all; ye'll sink clear through to Australia or some such place."

"And Daddy's car!" Dorinda cried. "Oh, he's going to be *furious!*" She still wore her mink jacket; it looked drowned.

"Isn't he insured against bogs?" Jonathan asked. "Do you fellows think you can get us out of here?"

"Ah, well, we might just be doing that," Paddy said. "Ye've a rope in your trunk, Tim?"

Tim was already opening the back of the car, brought out six fathoms of nylon warp. "It's useful," he explained at large. "For towing, ye know. Can ye take a line, Mr. Anders?"

It was already on its way. Jonathan caught it, passed it round Anna's waist, tied a bowline.

She smiled at him. "I'm not quite sure whether

217

I owe you my life yet again, Jonathan, seeing that it was you got me into this mess in the first place. And now we are both prisoners, and neither of us will get the formula." She sighed. "All this effort for nothing." She climbed down the back of the car. "All right, Mick."

They dragged her across the bog, and a few minutes later Jonathan stood beside her; they were both coated in mud, but otherwise unhurt. They watched the Rolls sinking lower into the mud.

"Is there nothing you can do?" Dorinda asked. "That rope . . ."

"Won't pull any Rolls out of that stuff," Tim said. "Ah, well, ye'll be wanting to go back to the castle, I suppose, Miss Wantage?"

"I suppose," she said. "I'd like to get rid of these filthy clothes. But what Papa is going to say . . ."

"And you'll return Madame Cantelna's three friends in due course, Mick?" Pete asked.

"Oh, sure, Mr. Rodgers. When ye and Mr. Anders have had time to catch your plane."

"I do not understand," Anna said. "Do you mean we are not under arrest?"

"*You* are," Pete said. "But only for twelve hours. Then you'll be welcome to go. In fact, I rather suspect these gentlemen will be happy if you do. Oh, before I forget . . ." he reached into the breast pocket of Anna's jacket, removed the little oilskin bag. "We'll have this little lot. And your pistol, if it's not too much trouble."

"I still do not understand," Anna said. "Are these foreign agents not your enemies, Mick?"

"Ah, well, Miss Cantelna," Mick explained. "The fact is, Mr. Rodgers and I got to chatting while we were waiting for the tide to go down, and it seems his aunt in Boston is my own aunt in Boston too. Sure, and I'm hoping to cross the water to see the old lady next year. Well, now, ye can't be expecting me to go fighting me own cousin?"

Anna looked scandalized. "And Mr. Anders? Don't you think he will tell the British authorities what happened here?"

"Sure and he's welcome," Mick said. "But the fact is, we got that shipment of rifles out, all right, and there won't be any more, because, ye see, the passage through the caves has collapsed. So as a gun-running center, Kiltone is just a piece of history. We'll be moving along. So Mr. Anders will have to come looking all over again."

Anna gazed at Jonathan. "You are not only talented. You are lucky as well." She shrugged. "Maybe our third meeting will be lucky for me."

Jonathan dressed slowly. He did not think he would ever feel rested again, but it made a lot of difference to be clean. He stood at the narrow window and watched the dawn trying to get up over the Kiltone hills. In another hour he'd be on a train down to Shannon, and home. It had been a hectic two days.

"I suppose I'd better have those papers," he said.

"They're probably better off with me." Pete knotted his tie.

"Now look here, old man," Jonathan said. "I

came here for them, remember? You only came to find out what the Russians were doing."

"Ah, well, as Mick would say, I'm afraid I wasn't quite truthful, Jonathan."

"Is that so?" Jonathan demanded. "Well, now, you just listen to me."

"Try this." Pete took an envelope from his pocket, handed it over.

It was addressed to Jonathan Anders, Esq. Jonathan opened it, stared at the single sheet of paper; he had already recognized the handwriting. "For the purposes of this exercise, Mr. Peter Rodgers is to be considered your superior officer." The signature was also unmistakable. "Harold Craufurd."

"You mean..."

"I mean our people asked for you, Jon, old man. The State Department has a long memory, several million of them. When we discovered that Anna Cantelna was heading the so-called journalistic mission to Kiltone, somebody remembered that she'd been in the British Isles on a previous occasion and had had a close run-in with a certain British agent. We couldn't remember his name, but when we contacted Whitehall they found it for us. You see, we had no idea at all what she was looking for, and as she had an invitation from Lord Wantage, she could have sat here all winter, patiently probing. We had to push her into action."

"For Heaven's sake," Jonathan said. "You mean I was the bait for *your* trap? I ought to smash you. You could have let on."

"I was advised against it. By Mr. Craufurd, as it

happens. I saw him just before coming over here, to learn what kind of a chap you were, and he said to let you have your head. 'He works best when he thinks it's all on his shoulders,' is what he said."

"The old buzzard," Jonathan said. "He's never given me that impression. Anyway, I'm not sure he's right. This one was rather a close call. I'm surprised you didn't have just a little insurance lurking behind a friendly bush."

"The fact is, we don't really have a lot of men in Eire," Pete admitted. "It's not what we would call a trouble spot, at least as regards to us. Anyway, I figured when the chips were down I'd be able to find some local help. After all, we speak the same language."

They took their bags downstairs to where Tim was waiting with the taxi. Dorinda was waiting too; she had changed back into her crimson dressing gown and seemed none the worse for her adventure.

"I think, after all your exertions, you need a good rest," she remarked. "You should stay here for a day or two, Jonathan. You don't have to worry about Papa. He's taken to bed, and Dr. Kelly says he's suffering from shock. He inherited that car from his father, you see."

"I'd love to stay, Dorinda, believe me," Jonathan said. "But I've a man waiting to see me. He always is. And besides—you can't really afford to become involved. Think of the cost in minks. And cars. And evening gowns."

Pete sat back with a sigh. "To the station, Tim,

me boy, and don't spare the horsepower. Nice-looking girl. Pity she's an oddball. Otherwise you and I might both be regular visitors to Kiltone."

"You mean you're coming back?" Jonathan asked.

Pete winked. "I'm a sucker for good cooking, remember?"

ABOUT THE AUTHOR

Born in Georgetown, Guyana, Christopher Nicole left school at sixteen, as he says, "to see something of life before settling down to write." And that's exactly what he's done. He first traveled up and down the West Indies and then made briefer visits to Great Britain, Scandinavia, Italy, Russia, Poland, and the United States. Only those places he has actually visited are used as the settings for his novels. A former banker, Mr. Nicole now devotes all his time to writing. OPERATION NEPTUNE is his third adventure story involving the British agent Jonathan Anders and follows his already successful OPERATION MANHUNT and OPERATION DESTRUCT. When not traveling, Mr. Nicole, his wife and four children make their home on the Isle of Guernsey in the English Channel.